CW00832140

CHECKMATE
A KILLER

VEGAS CHANTLY MYSTERY #1

KYLE OWENS

Checkmate a Killer © Copyright Kyle Owens, 2022

All rights reserved. Published by OffBeat Publishing, LLC.
No part of this publication may be reproduced, distributed, or transmitted
in any form or by any means, including photocopying, recording, or other
electronic or mechanical methods, without the prior written permission of
the publisher, except in the case of brief quotations embodied in critical
reviews and certain other noncommercial uses permitted by copyright law.
For Information regarding permissions, write to: OffBeatReads@pm.me

*This publication includes works of fiction. Any resemblance to actual events
or persons, living or dead, is entirely coincidental, a product of the author's
imagination, or used fictitiously.*

ISBN (Print): 978-1-950464-44-9
ISBN (eBook): 978-1-950464-24-1

O n the outskirts of Blue Falls, Georgia, in the Pine Sap Camper Park (which had the catchy slogan "Come and stick around"), Vegas Chantly was sound asleep in her nineteen seventy-two silver Airstream camper. It was set up on lot twenty-one and had a giant painting of Woody Woodpecker on the right rear quarter panel.

Inside, everything was nearly quiet, with only the whispers of bird calls intertwined with rustling leaves seeping through the thin walls. At seven o'clock, the radio came on and awakened the warm August morning.

"Good morning, sleepy heads. Here's your quick rundown of the news on this fine day. A body was found at the Rhinehouse Apartments complex on Fifth Street. The police said it appeared to have been accidental, and the case is closed. In literature, local professor Oliver Kimball's essay on how to feed the hungry through cannibalism has now won both a Nobel Prize and a Bram

Stoker Award. Also, it's National Pig Day. So go out there and eat a wiener, America! Last up is the weather forecast — like they're going to get that right — brought to you by Fitness Plus and Diet Center, located at the Plaza Shopping Mall right beside Big Tony's Pizza. Rear entrance advised. ..."

Vegas slowly opened her eyes, reached out with her left hand, and turned off the radio. The twenty-seven-year-old sat up in bed, her shoulder-length blond hair tangled and sticking up as if she had been shocked.

She rubbed her eyes with her fists, let out a big yawn like a lioness after eating a tourist, and suddenly noticed that standing at the foot of her bed was a short, redheaded round-on-both-ends woman with her hands on her hips and big, oval, black-framed eyeglasses perched on her nose.

"We need to continue our talk from last night," she said.

"Good lord, Mom. You scared me to death," Vegas said, her hand clutching her heart. "No wonder I never get the hiccups."

Vegas leaned against the back wall of the camper while she continued to try to rub the sleep from her eyes.

Vegas' mom, Eleanor, looked around the camper, shook her head, and said, "I can't believe my only child is living in a camper in a camper park. If your father was alive, he'd roll over in his grave."

Vegas cocked an eyebrow as she digested her mother's words. "I think you said that wrong, but I'm too sleepy to know for sure or not."

"Why don't you move back in with me? There's absolutely no reason for you to be living in a place like this," pleaded her mother.

"No," said Vegas as she stared up at the ceiling in despair. "Last night my answer was no, and it's the same today. Now if you'll excuse me, I really need some coffee. And maybe that guy who plays Thor on a sweet roll."

Vegas slowly slid out of bed. She was wearing an extra-large red T-shirt with a drawing of Frankenstein's monster printed on it, and a pair of gray jogging pants cut off at the knees. She made her way to the kitchen counter, which took all of two steps.

"Why don't you want to move back in with me?" her mother implored.

"Because you're crazy, Mom."

"You live in a camper and you call me crazy. Look around you, sweetie. It's obvious that the private investigator business isn't working out for you."

"I'm doing fine, Mom."

"Do you have any clients lined up?"

"Tons."

Eleanor shook her head. "I didn't know you measured clients by weight now."

"Okay, hundreds then."

"Hundreds?" asked a doubtful Eleanor. "Am I supposed to believe that you actually have hundreds of clients?"

Vegas got the coffee can off a shelf and began unscrewing the lid when the can slipped out of her hands, bounced off the floor, and sent coffee grounds everywhere.

"This morning isn't starting off well," Vegas said as she

bent down to pick up the can, and on her way back up hit her head on the underside of the counter, which sent her back to her knees.

"Ow. I think I'm dead," Vegas said as she rubbed her head. "I admit I could be off in my client count." She placed the can on the counter from her kneeling position and then used her hands to scoop the coffee off the floor and back into the can.

"You're not going to drink that are you?" her mother asked in a state of horror.

"It doesn't matter. I don't like this brand of coffee anyway," Vegas said.

"Are these clients ever going to pay you?"

"Stop worrying about my financial situation, Mom. The camper's paid for."

"Of course it's paid for. Your father paid it off in ninety-six."

Eleanor sat on the bed, shook her head, and tried to keep from crying as she said, "I just don't like you being a private investigator. It's dangerous, you know? If anything ever happened to you, I don't know what I would do. Well, I'd probably sell the camper."

Vegas began placing several fistfuls of coffee grounds into the machine. "Mom, I'll be okay. I'm a big girl now. I can iron my pants and everything."

Eleanor noticed some business cards on the tiny kitchen table. She picked them up and began shuffling through them as if they were playing cards.

"Vegas Chantly, pie? What's that?" Eleanor asked.

"That's P.I., Mom. This coffee maker isn't even working."

Eleanor reread the cards, "I need to get these glasses changed. Where did you get these?"

"Pepper made 'em for me on his computer," Vegas said as she walked to her tiny red refrigerator, opened the door, and retrieved a root beer. She popped open the can and took a big swig.

"Pepper? I'm not sure I like you hanging out with him."

"He's fine — in his own way."

"Doesn't he think he was once probed by aliens or something?"

"It could have happened," Vegas said with an unsure look on her face and took a seat in a patio chair pushed into the corner. It sat beneath a shelf that held a thirteen-inch black-and-white television from the nineteen-seventies and a Pink Panther plush toy.

"What's all this on the back of the cards?" asked Eleanor.

"Those are my rates."

"Do you think you can get that much just for looking into people's windows?"

"I do a little more than that. And yes, the rates are competitive."

Eleanor put the cards down, then turned to her daughter and asked in her serious voice, "I want you to be honest with me now. Do you need money?"

"I've got money, Mom," Vegas said as she drank her root beer.

"Oh, my God! Are you hooking?" Eleanor said as she threw her hands in the air in despair.

"Yeah, that's how I can afford all of this. Enough of this now, Mom. Every time we get together, you end up talking about me and my life. Let's talk about you for once. What's new with you?"

Eleanor appeared to be a bit taken aback by her daughter's query, "Me? What did you hear?"

"Nothing, Mom," Vegas said through a sigh as she stared at the ceiling, then back at her mother. "Just tell me what you did yesterday."

Eleanor's eyes indicated she was trying to retrace her life from yesterday. "Oh, the other day I was watching *The Wheel of Fortune,* and before the lady contestant said a letter, I yelled out S, and do you know that there were three S's in the puzzle? I was so excited. That's never happened to me before — or since, for that matter. But for one moment in a long day, I was Lady Action."

A proud look was etched on Eleanor's face as Vegas asked, "What was the answer?"

"Answer to what?"

"To the puzzle. What was the answer?" Vegas asked in a frustrated voice.

"I think it was Rain Maker or something like that," Eleanor said.

"There are no S's in Rain Maker."

"Well, Mommy can't remember what it was. I just remember being excited that I got the S's right. You know, if I'm ever on *The Wheel of Fortune,* that's going to be my strategy. I'm going to say, 'Give me an S, Alex.'"

"The name of the host is Pat."

"No, I'm pretty sure it's a man," Eleanor said.

"Whatever you say, Mom," Vegas said in surrender. "I'm going to regret asking this, but what if the contestant before you asks for an S?"

Eleanor thought it over, and a plan of strategy seemed to reveal itself to her satisfaction. "Well, I guess I'll go with R then, in case it's Rain Maker again. You know, I'm pretty good at these game shows during the day. My mind is always working. I'd love to be on one. Do they make you take a test first before you can be a contestant?"

"You better hope not," Vegas said.

The payphone situated beneath a large oak tree some twenty feet from Vegas' camper suddenly rang.

"I'll get it," Eleanor shouted as she rushed out of the camper.

"No, you won't!" Vegas yelled as she sat her can of root beer down and tried to beat her mother to the phone. The tail of her shirt caught on a sharp point on the tiny kitchen counter, and her mother made it to the phone as she finally freed herself.

"Hello? Yes, this is Vegas Chantly's residence. I'm her partner," Eleanor said, much to the chagrin of her daughter.

Vegas took the phone from her mother. "Give me that," she said to her. "And you're not my partner, you're my Brutus."

Vegas composed herself, then began speaking into what was probably the last payphone in all of Georgia — and perhaps in all of civilization.

"Yes, this is Vegas Chantly. I can do that. Give me your

address." Vegas then whispered to her mother, "Get me a pen and a piece of paper."

"Who is it?" asked Eleanor.

"Get me a pen and a piece of paper," repeated Vegas.

"Who is it?"

"Get me a pen and a piece of paper."

"But who is it?"

"Work with me here, woman," Vegas said in annoyance.

"Okay, okay," Eleanor mumbled as she reached into her purse and dug her hand into it like it was a backhoe. She somehow found a pen and a scrap of paper and handed them to Vegas.

"He's a chess champion?" Vegas continued as she spoke with the person on the other end of the line. "Wilson Hopkins. I think I heard about him on the news. Was he the one that played a whole class of second-graders and they tied him up and painted him purple? Interesting. Bosco Hopkins ... Rhinehouse Apartments ... Apartment fifteen. Okay. I'll be right there. Bye."

Vegas hung up the phone.

"Is that a new case?" asked Eleanor.

"Yeah. A chess champion died, and the police said it was an accident, but the brother believes he was murdered."

"Murdered?" Eleanor said in a voice drowned in worry.

"That's just what he thinks," Vegas said in an attempt to calm her mother's worries. "I'm sure the police were right in saying it was an accident."

"If you believe the police are right, then why are you taking the case?"

Vegas tried to deflect the question and mumbled, "I'm just curious, is all."

"You don't have any other cases lined up, do you?" Eleanor replied in what Vegas called her "interrogation tone."

"Everything's fine," Vegas said, hoping her mother would miraculously just move on. "I'm just going through a slow time right now. Not a lot of people need detectives in August. Solar wind patterns and all. Besides, maybe I'll learn about chess when I get there."

"You know, your father tried to teach me chess, but I was afraid of the horse."

"I really don't have time to try and understand you right now. I've got to go change," Vegas said as she headed back to the camper.

"We can take my vehicle," Eleanor said.

Vegas stopped at the camper door, turned to her mother, and shouted, "You're not coming with me!"

"I'll be your backup."

"I don't need a backup. I don't want you coming with me. That's final!"

"But your minivan is in the shop. Remember?"

Vegas' self-assurance seemed to collapse into itself when her mother reminded her of that fact. "I forgot about that. The battery wasn't charging."

"That's why I only drive vehicles that run on gas."

"I really wish you'd run away from my life," Vegas said.

Eleanor took Vegas by the hand, kissed it, stared into

her daughter's blue eyes, and said, "Mommy would never do that."

Depressed, Vegas went inside her camper, changed her clothes, combed her hair, and came out twenty minutes later to find Eleanor waiting for her by the door. She grabbed her daughter by the hand and led her to her ivory-colored GMC Yukon.

"This reminds me of my taking you to kindergarten class on your first day of school," Eleanor said with a smile.

"I'm going to investigate a possible murder. How does that remind you of taking me to my first day of kindergarten?"

"You weren't appreciative then either."

As they got in the car, Vegas picked up a book that was in the passenger's seat.

"What's this? D.B. Cooper? Why do you have a book about D.B. Cooper?"

"Now, I don't want to scare you, but I think your Uncle Ray was D.B. Cooper," Eleanor casually informed her as she slid her key into the ignition.

"I have an Uncle Ray?" Vegas asked with a snarled lip.

"You can call him D.B."

"What makes you think he's D.B. Cooper?"

"Honey, it has to be somebody."

"Being alive doesn't make you a D.B. Cooper suspect, Mom."

"He was in the military. He parachuted in the Navy."

"Was he a fighter pilot?"

"He was stationed on a submarine."

Vegas stared at her mother in disbelief and couldn't help but say, "He parachuted from a submarine?"

"It was very hush-hush."

"Sounds like it would be very drown-drown."

"I'm sure the government gave him an air tank and a fishing pole when he jumped."

Vegas cocked her elbow to rest it on the opened window, placed her head in her hand, and said, "That doesn't make any sense, Mom."

"Oh, it will. Believe me, I know what I'm doing," Eleanor said and started rummaging through her purse.

"What are you looking for?" Vegas asked.

"My keys."

"They're in the ignition, Mom."

"Oh, that's handy, isn't it?"

Vegas just shook her head and wondered, "How in the world did I ever get to kindergarten class on time?"

2

Eleanor pulled her SUV into the parking lot of the local shopping plaza. Vegas looked at Eleanor puzzled as her mother parked somewhat between two white lines and shoved the gear shift lever into park.

"I can't believe I found a parking spot so easily," Eleanor said with a big grin. "It usually takes me half an hour or—"

Vegas interrupted her mother. "Why did you bring me to Home Depot? Is this where Uncle Ray buried the money?"

Eleanor tried to calm her daughter's emotions as she touched her arm with her hand. "Mommy has to get a few things. Now, don't worry, it won't take me long, then I'll take you to your murder investigation."

Vegas placed her face into her hands and took several quick breaths before she ran her hands down her face as if her fingers were rain running down a window. Vegas stared at her mother and pleaded, "I'm on a case here. I told him that I was on my way. I have to get there now. I can't be late for the first meeting with my client — it's unprofessional. I don't have time for you to go shopping."

"I'll just be a minute. I need to get some fertilizer for my flowers."

"Fertilizer?" Vegas shot back. "You're stopping here for fertilizer when I have to get to my case?"

Eleanor again tried to calm her daughter with some soothing words that only a mother could muster. "It'll be okay. Honest. I know where it is, and I'll go in there, pick it up, check out, then boom, I'm back in the SUV with my daughter. This is the only place that sells this fertilizer, and it works fantastic. You should see the size of my cucumbers. They look like pumpkins. Well, they're not orange. Sometimes when they go bad they turn orange. I meant in their size, they are like pumpkins. I guess I should have compared them to watermelons since watermelons are green, too."

Vegas just stared out the front windshield with a blank look on her face.

"The name of it is Henderson Natural Fertilizer, in case you want to get you some. Did you ever hear their ad?"

Eleanor's ramblings made Vegas feel like she was five years old and her mother was trying to convince her that the doctor's office was really the home of Big Bird. She softly said, "No, I've never heard their ad before."

"We put the 'Mmmmm' in manure. I think that's so cute. Are you going in with me?"

"No."

"You can't wait out here, you'll get hot. Come on in with Mommy, and it'll help me shop faster."

"I can't believe how this day is going," Vegas said as she looked out the passenger's-side window and saw a teenage boy trying to wrangle up the shopping carts to take them back inside the store.

"It's special to me, too, honey," Eleanor said.

Vegas felt like she was on a mule that wouldn't do anything she wanted it to, so she just surrendered to the chaos of the moment and agreed to go with her mother. "I'll go with you so we can get this done fast. But we have to hurry. Do you understand that?"

"I'll go so fast your head will spin, I promise."

Eleanor got out of the vehicle, and Vegas reluctantly followed as they made their way inside the Home Depot.

Eleanor retrieved a shopping cart and pushed it only a couple of feet when she stopped.

"Let's go, let's go," Vegas spurred her on.

"Oh, this one has a bad wheel. I always get the one with the bad wheel, and everybody can hear me all over the store. I once had a cart that the wheel broke completely off, and I knocked over a whole display of hemorrhoid medicine," Eleanor said as she took the cart back and began trying the others.

"I doubt people hearing you all over the store had anything to do with a bad wheel or hemorrhoids," Vegas said.

"What did you say, honey?"

"We have to hurry, Mom," pleaded Vegas.

"We just came into the store, honey. I have to get a good

cart or Mommy will veer into a stack of lumber, and you know how long that will take us to clean up."

"This can't be happening," Vegas said.

"I know, I know, you have a case. I'll just get the fertilizer and then we'll be off to murder and mayhem."

Eleanor took another cart and pushed it back and forth and said, "This one is perfect. It's in the Goldilocks zone. Do you need to go to the bathroom? I know where it is, but you shouldn't sit all the way down on the seat, just to be safe. You don't know who was in there before you showed up. I always stand when I use a public restroom. That's why they won't let me use the restroom at Burger King anymore."

"I'm going to go wait in the car and pray to be kidnapped," Vegas said as she started back toward the vehicle.

"Mommy will hurry!" Eleanor shouted. People looked up from their shopping to see what was going on. "Remember to let the window down, or you'll get hot and get that rash on your bottom!"

Now it seemed like everyone in the store was staring at Vegas, and without missing a beat, she yelled, "Oh, like I'm the only one that happens to."

Vegas made her way to the vehicle, got in, slammed the door shut, and waited and waited and waited until some forty minutes later her mother came out with a full cart.

"Did she buy the whole store out?" Vegas asked herself. Her mother waved, and Vegas just rolled her eyes. She got out to assist with the bags and asked, "What took you so long?"

Eleanor opened the rear hatch and told her daughter, "My credit card wasn't working when I slid it through their thingamajig. And do you know why? It had peanut butter on it! Now where I got peanut butter, I got no idea," she said with a laugh.

Vegas was putting the bags into the back of the vehicle as fast as she could when her mother said, "You go ahead and put the fertilizer up. I've got to go next door to the supermarket and get me a can of green beans."

Vegas turned quickly to her mother and shouted, "No, no, no! I've got a case I've got to get to!"

"Mommy will hurry."

"You said that forty minutes ago, and you're still not through shopping yet. Can't you do this later?"

Eleanor just kept walking away as she shouted, "It won't take long! I just need to get a can of green beans."

"You said all you needed here was a bag of fertilizer, and you came out with a whole cart full of things."

"I can't pass up a sale, honey; that's not good money management. Now, Mommy loves you, and I promise to hurry. How's your bottom?" Eleanor asked.

"My bottom's fine, Mom!"

"It's just that I know it's hot out here, and you've been in the car and—"

"Just get your beans so we can leave!" Vegas shouted as she noticed a mother and her three kids staring at them. She was so embarrassed, it was like she was in a dream in which she was at school and only now realized she wasn't wearing any pants.

Vegas put her right hand to the side of her face, trying

to hide from the mother and her kids, and went back to loading the vehicle.

"You load the stuff in the vehicle and I'll run and get my green beans. I'll hurry. You can time me if you want. Ready, go!" Eleanor shouted as she wobbled as fast as she could toward the supermarket but had to stop to rest after about ten feet.

Vegas shook her head, then finished loading the purchases into the SUV, took the cart to the corral in the middle of the parking lot, and then sat in the vehicle and stewed. "Just drive away, Vegas," she mumbled. "That's all you have to do. She wouldn't mind." She thought it over and said, "No, she would mind. I have her manure."

Vegas looked at her watch impatiently every couple of minutes for the next half hour, until Eleanor finally arrived — with four plastic bags of groceries.

Vegas leaned over and opened the driver's-side door, and Eleanor handed the bags to Vegas and got into the driver's seat.

"I am not as young as I want to be, that's for sure," Eleanor said as she tried to catch her breath. "It sure was crowded in there. Don't people work anymore? I got a good cart though."

"I thought you went in there for green beans," Vegas said as she looked through the plastic bags.

"They had a great deal on fish sticks."

Vegas looked in the bag and pulled out the *Guinness Book of World Records*.

"Why did you buy the *Guinness Book of World Records*?"

"I'm thinking of entering it."

"What on Earth for?"

"I want to make my mark on the world," Eleanor said as she slammed the door shut, catching her seatbelt in the door frame. She opened it back up, cleared her seatbelt, and continued where she had left off. "You know, leave a legacy. Right now all I'm known for is birthing you and having peanut butter on my credit card. You know, I was reading it in the checkout line, and they had a picture of this man that juggled eighteen bricks. That's probably how he got that cut on his head. I know it's an odd talent, but it's very inspirational. Oh, and I got you a dozen eggs. Now, I know they're brown, but you still have to cook 'em."

Vegas looked into the bag again and pulled out a very large box of fish sticks and read the box out loud: "'Jonah's Fish Sticks. We know seafood from the inside out.' This is a box of four hundred fish sticks. Why would anybody need four hundred fish sticks?"

"Deal of the century isn't it? Now Mommy will take you to your case. Oh, but I have a hair appointment—"

"No, Mom! There's not going to be any hair appointment!"

Eleanor realized that Vegas was fuming mad and said, "That's fair. I'll get it done another time. Tina will understand."

Vegas wanted to ignore the obvious, but she simply couldn't. "If you ever take me to my case, won't these fish sticks thaw before you get home?"

Eleanor looked at her in shock.

Thirty minutes later, Vegas was sitting in Eleanor's

CHECKMATE A KILLER   19

vehicle in her driveway. Eleanor came running out of the house, opened the vehicle door and got in, and immediately jumped back out and began hurrying toward the house.

"What's wrong now?" screamed Vegas.

"I forgot my purse! I'll be right back."

A minute later, Eleanor got back in the vehicle, her purse tucked securely under her arm.

"Do you want something to eat before we go?" Eleanor asked.

"Let's just go!" Vegas shouted in desperation.

"Gotcha," Eleanor said.

Eleanor backed out of the driveway but cut her wheels too soon and ran over the curb. The SUV made a loud thud as it backed onto the main avenue.

"I hope that wasn't somebody," Eleanor said as she drove Vegas to her case at the Rhinehouse Apartments.

3

Vegas and her mother walked into the foyer of the Rhinehouse Apartments on the backside of the noon hour. The sun was shining through the glass door, which caused bright patterned streaks on the black-speckled floor. To the right was a small office with a sign over the door that read "Security." It wasn't the best-looking apartment building they had seen before, but they had seen worse.

"I can't believe how long it took us to get here," said a frustrated Vegas.

"I know. The traffic was terrible," Eleanor replied as she stared out the window toward the street.

Vegas let out a sound like that of a little boy pretending to be a tractor. "That's not what I was referring to, and you know it. We should have been here a couple of hours ago, but you had to go shopping for poop."

"It was natural fertilizer, not poop. Now, Mommy did

the best she could do. I shopped harder than I ever shopped before so we could get here on time, and this is the thanks I get."

"You shouldn't have been shopping at all."

Eleanor mumbled, "I'm sorry. It's just that I'm new at the private investigator business."

Vegas became incensed and said, "You're not in the private investigator business! You're in the driving-your-daughter-crazy business. And I must say that you're very good at it."

They were both quiet for a few seconds as a woman in her thirties came down the stairs. She had obviously overheard their arguing and now looked at the two of them confusedly.

"Hello," Vegas said.

"It's a nice day isn't it?" added Eleanor. "Unless of course, you're with your daughter."

The person smiled as she began to walk out the door when Eleanor asked, "Do you have children?"

The woman was surprised by her question and said, "No."

"Well, when you do, don't drive 'em to work."

The woman didn't understand but just smiled and walked out the door, happy to be away from the two of them.

"You realize that woman thinks we're crazy," Vegas said.

"Why are you yelling at me in the foyer of an apartment building? This isn't how your father and I raised you."

"I'm yelling at you in an apartment building foyer because that's where we are. I can't wait to get my vehicle back out of the shop so you can go back to your world of game shows, and I can go back to my world of work."

Eleanor thought about what her daughter said, then replied, "Maybe you should just sell the minivan and get another one. But get something big enough for your future kids."

"I don't have any money to get another vehicle, and I'm not interested in kids right now. Raising you is hard enough," Vegas said.

"You should get a vehicle like mine. A big SUV so you're safe in case of an accident or something. I had it tuned up a few weeks ago. Did you notice how much power it had?"

"Oh, yeah, everything you hit fell down," Vegas said. "Now let's go."

The two of them walked toward the stairs when an attractive Hispanic man came around the corner carrying a mop and bucket. His hair was jet black, and he wore tight jeans and a dark long-sleeve shirt with the sleeves rolled up past his large biceps.

Eleanor bumped her daughter's arm and raised her eyebrows as she nodded in the direction of the man, an indication that she should stop what she was doing and marry him on the spot.

"Stop it," Vegas whispered to her mother before turning to the handsome janitor and asking, "Excuse me, but could you tell us where apartment fifteen is?"

"Apartment fifteen?" he queried back at them as if he

CHECKMATE A KILLER 23

was surprised. "Are you with the police?"

"Private investigator," Vegas said as she pulled out a business card that Pepper had made for her and handed it to the janitor.

He looked at it and said, "Vegas Chantly, Pie."

"That's P.I. How is everybody getting pie out of that?" Vegas asked.

"She's single," said Eleanor, which brought a stare from Vegas that contained horror and anger strangled together.

Vegas then pretended that her mother was a potted plant, so as to ignore her, and turned back to the janitor and said, "We didn't catch your name."

"Billy Sanchez. So you're a private investigator?" he asked as he stared at the card.

"Yes," Vegas said.

"Apartment fifteen? I suppose you're here about the Wilson Hopkins accident."

"Yes."

"I thought he just tripped and hit his head on something. What's to investigate?"

"His brother just has some questions he wants answered," Vegas said.

"Oh. Well, I'll show you where the apartment is, then. Just follow me."

"You can just give us directions, then we won't bother you further," Vegas said.

"Let him show us if he wants to," Eleanor replied. She was trying her best to get a relationship going between the two of them.

"That's okay, I don't mind," Billy assured them. "I've

got to go up to room ten and unclog the toilet again, and I'm not looking forward to it. That's the third time this week. This wouldn't keep happening if they'd eat right. Every janitor within twenty blocks sure wishes that Taco Palace would shut down. They're working us to death."

"Maybe they're in cahoots with the plumber's union," Vegas suggested. "Say, did you see anything suspicious the night of Wilson's death?"

"No, I didn't work that night."

"Are you married?" asked Eleanor, which brought a sharp glance from Vegas.

"No, I'm not married."

"Where were you that night?" Vegas asked.

"I'd rather not say."

"It would be helpful if you would," said Vegas, curious as to why he didn't want to tell her.

"What was the guy's name again we're investigating?" Eleanor whispered to Vegas.

"Wilson Hopkins," Vegas said.

Eleanor stared at the janitor and asked point blank, "Did you kill Wilson Hopkins?"

"Mom!" Vegas said in horror.

"What? I didn't kill anybody, lady," Billy said.

"Aha!" Eleanor shouted as she pointed her finger at Billy.

"Why are you pointing at me?" Billy asked.

"Mom, go back to the vehicle. Or maybe Des Moines or something."

"Why else won't you tell us where you were if you didn't do it?" asked Eleanor. "Okay, okay. I tried out Taco Palace, if you have to know. Are you happy now? And don't you judge me!" Billy said emotionally and headed up the stairs.

"That went well," Eleanor said.

"Oh, yes, perfectly," Vegas replied as she and her mother followed Billy.

They followed Billy down the narrow upstairs hallway and stopped in front of a white door with a cheap gold-colored fifteen nailed to it, the kind you could get at any hardware store in the world.

"This is the apartment," Billy said.

"Did you know Wilson at all?" Vegas asked.

"A little bit. He liked chess. And well, I don't like to talk ill of the dead, but he was a bit annoying," Billy said.

"I know all about annoying," said Vegas, which brought a sharp look from Eleanor this time. "In what way?"

"He kept challenging me to chess games. I'd tell him I didn't know how to play or didn't have the time, and he would make fun of me. You know, putting me down by saying I was scared and a big baby, like something a kid would say. I don't know how to play chess, plus I had work to do. I didn't have the time to play some dumb board game."

The three of them stood there silently for a moment, then Billy asked, "Do you all need anything else?"

"No. Thank you for showing us to the apartment," Vegas said.

"Any time," Billy said with a smile. "If you need anything else, Miss Chantly, just let me know."

"Thank you," Vegas said with a slight blush as she watched him walk away.

"You should marry him," whispered Eleanor.

"Now?"

"Well, it's not like you're even trying. When was the last time you even went on a date?"

"I'm on a case right now, and when I'm on a case with you, I get to be the mom. Got it?" Vegas said.

"It wouldn't hurt you to go on one date. I could sign you up on one of those dating sites, and you'd be married by the end of the month."

"I'm not dating anything that comes out of a computer. Now concentrate on the case, not my love life. What am I saying? You should go back to the vehicle."

"You might need my help."

"You don't help. You interfere."

"I call it bonding."

"I don't want my mother coming on a case with me."

"Then it isn't your day, is it?"

Vegas seethed but decided they could argue about this another time. She then raised her arm to knock on the door when Eleanor grabbed her hand, pulling it down.

"What are you doing?" said a perplexed Vegas.

"Shouldn't we stand to the side in case someone inside shoots at us?"

"Who is going to shoot at us? Did you not pay for the tuneup or something?"

"That's the way they do it on cop shows."

"We're not cops. We're a private investigator and a crazy lady."

"Mommy doesn't think you're crazy."

Vegas sighed loudly and knocked on the door. A few seconds passed, and the door opened slightly, the chain lock still attached. Through the small opening, she saw a man in his thirties. He was slightly built, had short hair, wore round glasses, and had on a blue shirt that had what appeared to be a picture of the Star Trek Enterprise printed on it. He didn't say anything, just stared at them, looking Vegas and her mother over like they were a bad art exhibit.

Vegas momentarily lost her voice and all three of them stood silently, looking for all the world like they just discovered that their blind date was the ugliest person in the world.

Vegas cleared her throat and asked, "Are you Bosco Hopkins?"

"Password?" he asked bluntly.

Vegas and her mother looked at each other with confused expressions.

"Uh ... I'm supposed to meet a Bosco Hopkins here about a possible murder investigation concerning his brother," Vegas informed him. "There was no mention of a password or crazy people."

The guy continued staring and finally whispered, "Rumpelstiltskin." He then closed the door.

Vegas and her mother again looked at each other with confused expressions.

Eleanor shrugged and said, "It never hurts to have a security system."

"Then you shouldn't be blabbing the password out to the first two chicks that come to the door."

Vegas knocked on the door again. The same strange man opened it an inch and said, "Rumpelstiltskin."

"Um, aren't we supposed to say that part?" Vegas said.

The gentleman looked annoyed and closed his eyes for a second, then said, "Man, we have to do it again."

"Can't we just come in?" Vegas pleaded.

"No," the man replied. "We have to do this right or it doesn't count." He closed the door again.

Vegas looked at her mother and said, "I'm guessing we're going to be here a while."

"I'm kind of pumped about going inside," Eleanor said.

"Pumped?"

"I spend my days watching game shows. This is very exciting for me. You got murder and passwords — I see how you can get seduced into this business."

Vegas knocked again. The door was opened by the same bizarre man.

"Rumpelstiltskin," Vegas said in an unenthusiastic voice.

The man unlocked the chain, pulled open the door, and did Spock's Vulcan hand greeting with his right hand. Eleanor did one in return.

"I love *Star Trek,* too," Eleanor said. "Remember when Spock defeated Darth Vader?"

Eleanor walked into the apartment while the man stood there doing the Vulcan sign, waiting for Vegas to return the gesture.

"I can do this all day," warned the man.

Vegas surrendered and gave the Vulcan sign to him.

"You may enter," the man said.

"Gene Roddenberry ruined the world," Vegas said as she walked inside the apartment and closed the door behind her.

4

Vegas and Eleanor stood in the small living room of the small apartment. It consisted of the basics. There was a couch, which had tears in the blue cloth covering, perched beneath a small window containing a butterfly sticker in the lower left corner. Beside it was an end table with a lamp shaped like the USS Enterprise. The kitchen had large brown cabinets that hovered over a bar so that whoever was in the kitchen would have to bend their knees like a baseball umpire to speak to the people in the living room. A closed door that was probably a closet stood by the front entrance, and a shelf full of trophies was between the front entrance and the presumed closet. A door toward the back of the apartment stood open, and a single bedroom that had a bathroom across from it was visible. The floor was green and gold shag carpeting, which instantly reminded Vegas of an *Austin Powers* movie. The apartment was very clean and orderly.

"I want to thank you two for coming," said the man. "I'm Bosco Hopkins."

"It's our pleasure. I love your place. It's very masculine," Eleanor said. "It's nice to be in a home without wheels."

"Mom," Vegas said in a scolding manner.

"Thank you," said Bosco. "This isn't my apartment though, this is my brother's. I've come down here every day since his—" At this point, Bosco tried to keep from crying and excused himself. He went to the kitchen to compose himself out of their sight.

Eleanor leaned over to Vegas and whispered, "Should we search him?"

"For what?" replied Vegas.

"I don't know. I thought you'd done this before."

"I have. But what are we going to search him for?" asked Vegas.

"To see if he has any fingerprints?"

Vegas blankly gazed into her mother's eyes and stated, "I'm pretty sure that he has fingerprints."

Eleanor thought it over and asked, "So he did it?"

"No. For a girl who watches so much *Wheel of Fortune,* your investigative skills are a bit disappointing."

They heard Bosco blow his nose.

Eleanor said, "I think we should search him."

Bosco came back into the room. Vegas whispered to Eleanor, "I don't want to really touch him."

Bosco looked at Eleanor and asked, "Are you Vegas?"

"No, I'm Eleanor. This is Vegas here," she said as she pointed at her daughter. "I'm just her mother and driver."

Bosco asked Vegas, "Is this take-your-mother-to-work day or something?"

"Oh, that sounds interesting," said Eleanor. "We should do that sometime, honey."

"We do that every day," replied Vegas.

Bosco looked at them warily and asked Vegas, "Is this your first case?"

"No, it's not my first case," Vegas said in an offended tone. "Here's my card. My rates are on the back."

He took the card but didn't look at it. "I'd really prefer an investigator with more experience," he said.

"This isn't my first case. I've been doing this for a while now, and I'm very good at it," Vegas stated unapologetically.

Bosco replied, "I just thought maybe you brought your mother along because it was your first case."

"We're actually more like sisters than mother and daughter," Eleanor said. "People are always telling us that."

"I would define it more like a hostage situation," Vegas retorted.

Bosco asked, "Could you explain why your mother is here then?"

"Like all daughters, I can't explain my mother," Vegas confessed.

They all stared at each other blankly for a few moments.

"Let's start over again," Vegas suggested.

"Rumplestiltskin," Eleanor said.

"Not that far back, Mom."

"I'm Bosco Hopkins. No wait, I think I said that

already. Maybe we should go back outside and come back in again."

"No!" Vegas cried out as if pleading for mercy.

"Okay, uh, did you have any trouble finding the apartment?" Bosco asked. "Or did I already ask that?"

"No, the janitor showed us where to go," Eleanor said.

"Which one?"

"Billy Sanchez," Vegas said. "You have more than one janitor that works here?"

"Yeah. I think the other guy is family or close friends with the building owner. But I haven't seen him for a few days now. If you want anything done around here, you're better off getting Sanchez."

"Well, we didn't see the other one," Vegas said.

"Did you notice Sanchez's hat?" Bosco asked.

"He wasn't wearing a hat," Vegas said.

"That's odd," said Bosco. "He always wears a hat that says, 'I'm Squirrely for Shirley.'"

"Who's Shirley?" asked Eleanor.

"His hat," Bosco said.

"His hat is named Shirley?" Vegas asked.

"Yeah."

"Maybe you shouldn't marry him," Eleanor said in a whisper to her daughter.

"I wasn't going to marry him to start with," Vegas whispered back.

"I'm not married," Bosco said.

"I'm not surprised," Vegas said without any hesitation.

"I'll have you know that I dated Julia Roberts briefly," Bosco said in a serious tone.

"How briefly?" asked Vegas.

"I asked her out and she said no." And under his breath, he mentioned casually, "Then there were some court papers."

A long pause ensued, then Eleanor thought it best to fill the silence with talk of any sort: "When I was little, I had a pet chicken named Fido."

Vegas looked at her mother and shook her head.

"Why are you bringing that up?" Vegas asked angrily, the words coming out of her mouth like puffs of smoke.

"Nobody was saying anything, so I thought I would," Eleanor said. "It's just small talk to get something going. I'm great at small talk."

"I'm going to have to say no to that," warned Vegas.

"Isn't Fido a dog's name?" asked Bosco.

"Oh, he acted just like a dog," Eleanor said. "He would play fetch, lick you in the face and fly around the backyard."

"Dogs can't fly," Vegas said.

"Well, this one could," Eleanor said as she nodded her head and folded her arms into themselves as if she had just proven an obscure scientific theory.

Vegas stared at her mother and then at Bosco and wondered if they were the two strangest people she'd ever met in her life. Unfortunately, she had to admit that they weren't.

"Let's get back to the case," Vegas said with a handclap.

"I called you because my brother was murdered," Bosco said.

"But you said over the phone that the police declared it an accident," Vegas reminded him.

"They said it was an accident, but I know better," Bosco said as he pointed his finger at his head for emphasis.

"Tell me how you found your brother," Vegas said.

"Don't get too graphic, though," said Eleanor. "I'm still nauseous about my daughter not being married yet."

"You're going to bring that up now?" Vegas asked.

"It appears I'm going to have to bring it up quite a bit for the foreseeable future."

"I would like to restate that I'm not married," Bosco volunteered as he held up his ringless finger.

"Enough about marriage," said a vexed Vegas. "Now tell me how you found your brother."

"I came down on Saturday at seven in the morning—" said Bosco, but before he finished, Vegas interrupted.

"Down? You live in the building?"

"I live in the apartment right above here," Bosco said and pointed at the ceiling. "Apartment thirty."

"How cute," Eleanor replied. "It's like you're sleeping in bunk beds."

"We did have bunk beds when we were young, but they kept falling over. They had been recalled, but nobody told us. That's how I got this scar on my chin," he said as he boldly stuck his chin out for them to see before he continued, "and my fear of people jumping on top of me with their beds."

Eleanor stared at him and asked, "Wouldn't you see them coming?"

"We're getting too easily distracted here," Vegas said as

she turned back to Bosco. "Saturday morning at seven, when you came down, did you let yourself into his apartment?"

"Yes. The door was unlocked, and that was not like my brother at all. Especially on Saturday, because that's when he vacuums, and he keeps the door locked when he vacuums because he's afraid someone will come in and track up the floor before it settles good."

"Settles good?" asked Vegas.

"He had his ways."

"Where did you find your brother when you came in?" Vegas asked.

Bosco pointed to a place on the floor beside the trophy shelf. "Right here on the floor. He had several of his chess trophies on top of him. The police said that he tripped over the thick shag carpeting, hit his head on the wall, and the trophies fell off the shelf and onto him, killing him by striking him in the head. But I know that's not true because he always sets his trophies on the floor when he vacuums so he can get all the shelves clean. So they couldn't have fallen on him. Also, one of his trophies is missing."

"Are you positive it couldn't have just been an accident?" Vegas asked.

"It's impossible."

Vegas walked to the trophy shelf and immediately felt something on the floor that didn't feel right.

"There's a high spot here. The plywood underneath is raised up. This makes it seem like he could have tripped," Vegas said, observing the scene. "Then he would have fallen right into the shelf over here, and knocked the trophies down on him."

"I disagree," Bosco said. "He would have known about that spot and wouldn't have fallen."

Vegas looked at the trophies. "You say one of the trophies is missing?"

"Yes. And it's the biggest one, too," replied Bosco.

"Hmm … if it was an accident, then who would take it?" asked Vegas.

"Exactly," Bosco said.

"And you told the police this?"

"I didn't realize it was missing until today."

Vegas asked Bosco, "What kind of injury did your brother have?"

"It was a very bad head wound."

Vegas looked at the wall of trophies as she said, "I don't know if he could get a bad head wound from a trophy simply falling on him. … Maybe he hit his head on the wall and *that* caused his death, and the trophies falling on him really didn't have anything to do with it."

Eleanor began walking about the apartment. She stopped at the trophy case and took her hands and placed her thumbs together, raising her fingers so as to peer through the open space above the thumbs, as if she was looking through a camera. "I don't believe it either," she said.

"But it does sound plausible that he could have stumbled, hit the wall, and the trophies hit him in a bad place on the head and killed him," Vegas considered.

"But a man vacuuming? I don't think so."

"What were you doing with your hands just now anyway?" asked Vegas.

"Monk does it all the time," Eleanor said. "I was becoming one with Bosco when he died."

"Wilson," Vegas reminded her. "His name was Wilson. Bosco is alive and standing over there in front of us thinking of nursery rhyme passwords."

Eleanor looked at Bosco and then back at Vegas and said, "I'm going to have to do it again then."

Eleanor started up the routine with her imaginary camera, but Vegas grabbed her by the arm, pulled her back, and turned to Bosco. "Do you remember anything else that might indicate he was murdered?"

"There's also this," Bosco said as he walked to a large answering machine that looked like a relic from ancient times. Vegas and her mother looked at it in confusion.

"I heard a disturbing voice on his answering machine," Bosco said.

"What year is this thing?" Vegas asked as she noted its hulking size.

"Nineteen seventy-three," Bosco said. "It belonged to our parents. He inherited it when they passed, and I got the dog's yellow ball."

"We used to have an answering machine similar to that, but I broke it trying to kill a grasshopper," Eleanor said.

Vegas stared at her mother and asked, "And you're mentioning this for what reason?"

"I thought it might help with the investigation. You know, personal experiences," replied Eleanor.

Vegas shook her head, turned back to Bosco, and asked, "Why didn't he get a new answering machine?"

"Oh, my brother didn't believe in technology."

"But an answering machine is technology," Vegas said.

Bosco stood silent for a moment before he said, "Well, you've got me there. But listen to this message. When I heard it, my blood ran cold."

Bosco hit play on the answering machine and his voice could be heard clearly, saying, "Did you get them wieners?"

Bosco immediately turned it off and said, "Oh, that was me. Sorry. I went back too far. I didn't mean it in a threatening way, either."

He fast-forwarded to the next message, and a much more ominous voice spoke. "I'm going to get you, chess man," it said.

"That does sound menacing," Eleanor said.

"Did you share this with the police?" Vegas asked.

"I called them and told them about it, but I accidentally played them the wiener message and they hung up on me."

"Why didn't you call back?"

"I tried, but they thought I was joking around."

"Did your brother ever tell you that he was being threatened?" Vegas asked.

"No. But chess is one of the dark arts."

"It is?" Vegas asked in an unbelieving voice.

"We have to checkmate a killer," Eleanor said.

Vegas shook her head in disbelief. "Really?"

"Hey, that's pretty good," Bosco said. "Now I see why you bring your mother on your cases."

"Thank you," Eleanor said. "It's nice to be appreciated for once."

Vegas turned back to Bosco and asked, "Was there someone in the chess world that might want him dead?"

"Everyone was jealous of my brother because of his skill. He was also a bestselling author: *Winning Chess through Diet, Strategy, and Hypnotism.* It sold forty-two copies in only six months. That's pretty good for a chess book."

Vegas couldn't help but ask, "How do you win chess through hypnotism?"

Bosco stood rigid and proceeded to stare intently at Vegas in an apparent attempt to hypnotize her.

"I should have asked about the diet part," Vegas said as she began to feel uncomfortable with Bosco's unrelenting gaze.

Eleanor resumed walking around the apartment. She came to the closet near the entry door and opened it. It was a simple four-by-four-foot room with a single light bulb in the middle of the ceiling. Inside were a vacuum cleaner, a box fan, a small shelf on the right side sparsely filled with the usual home items, and a box of clothes on the other side of that. Eleanor noticed a hat lodged behind the box and grabbed it. On it was written, "I'm Squirrely for Shirley."

"Oh, my goodness!" Eleanor said, which got the attention of Vegas and broke the trance of Bosco.

"What did you find?" Vegas asked as she looked at the hat in her mother's hand.

"That's the janitor's hat," Bosco said. "It's the one Billy

Sanchez always wears and that all the girls go all goo-goo eyes over."

"I don't think they're goo-goo eyeing his hat," Vegas said.

"Yeah they are, I've seen it," Bosco said.

"That's the first clue I've ever found!" Eleanor gushed. "I feel like a *CSI* detective right now."

"Why would that be in there?" wondered Bosco.

"Do you think your brother might have stolen it from the janitor?" Vegas asked.

"My brother is a decent man. He'd never steal anything from anyone. He might hypnotize you, but he would never steal from you."

"Would he have had the janitor up here to fix something?" asked Vegas.

"There's nothing to fix in the closet," Bosco said.

"Maybe the light?"

Eleanor turned the light on and off several times before it got on Vegas' nerves.

"That's enough, Mom."

"Either there was nothing wrong with the light or he fixed it," Eleanor said. "You know, my TV in the guest bedroom doesn't work either."

"Well, I'm not going to spend the night until you get it fixed," Vegas said as she leaned into the closet. "I don't see any water leaks that might require any maintenance. Did the police look in here?"

"I don't know," said Bosco. "When they came in, I stayed outside. I was too disturbed to be in here then."

"It was behind the box, so maybe they didn't see it," Eleanor said.

"Or maybe they saw it but didn't think it meant anything," Vegas replied.

"Are you all going to take my case?" Bosco asked.

"Yes, we will," Eleanor said. "And if we don't solve your brother's death, then that means it never happened."

Vegas stared at her mother. "That slogan isn't going to work in the detective field."

Vegas turned to Bosco and asked, "Are you the one who called the police first?"

"Yes. As soon as I found my brother lying on the floor, I called nine-one-one, and they sent an ambulance and a police car."

Vegas looked at the answering machine and asked, "Can I borrow your answering machine?"

"I'll answer your calls for you, honey," Eleanor said.

Vegas rolled her eyes and said, "I want to take it to the police to listen to. I doubt they have a cassette player down there, so I'll need to take the machine with me."

"Sure, you can take it. But what about Sanchez? Should I hypnotize him or something?" asked Bosco.

"No, don't go hypnotizing anybody. We're not sure about anything just yet," Vegas said.

"Don't worry, Bosco. You hired the right private investigator when you hired Vegas Chantly. My daughter is full of spunk and independence."

"Thanks, Mom. Can you drive me to the station?"

"Of course," Eleanor said, and the two headed out with the answering machine.

V egas and Eleanor walked into the Blue Falls
Police Station at one-thirty. Vegas was toting the
victim's heavy answering machine in her arms,
trying to shift its weight from side to side in an attempt to
maintain a positive grip.

The station was busy, and everyone that worked there
ignored them. Eleanor looked them all over and made a
motherly observation: "Not much husband material in
here, is there?"

"Mom, not now," Vegas said as she shifted the
answering machine up toward her shoulders for a better
grip.

"I don't want to sound mean, but the only thing worth
doing in here is aerobics," Eleanor pointed out.

Vegas stared at her mother and shook her head as they
walked to a policeman who looked relatively unbusy. Vegas
asked, "Who's in charge here?"

"That would be Sergeant Miller," he said without

looking up from his computer screen. Vegas and Eleanor stood waiting for more information, and he glanced up and saw Vegas struggling with the bulky machine. "But he's not interested in buying any electronics."

"Oh, I'm not selling—"

"He thinks the internet is just a fad," the policeman interrupted before Vegas could finish her sentence.

"We just want to talk to him about our Hopkins case," Eleanor said.

"What Hopkins case?" asked the policeman. "Are you two detectives or something?"

Eleanor began to explain. "See this man fell down and hit his head, well, at least that's what the police think, but his brother thinks he was murdered because of the hat I found and—"

"He was killed with that record player?" asked the policeman.

"No. That's an answering machine," Eleanor said. "See, well, I think it would be best to start from the beginning. The password was Rumpelstiltskin, and—"

"Mom!" Vegas interrupted and addressed the policeman. "Could you just tell us if Sergeant Miller is in?" She shifted the weight of the answering machine to her right side, looking as if she was ready to have her pig judged at the county fair.

"He's in his office. You go through that door over there," the policeman said and pointed at the door.

"Thank you," Vegas said and headed toward the sergeant's office.

"By the way, which dwarf was Rumpelstiltskin anyhow?" whispered Eleanor.

"Maybe you should wait outside," Vegas suggested.

"Outside? Where outside?"

"I don't know, Utah maybe."

Vegas tried to knock on the door but was having problems doing so without dropping the answering machine.

"Do you want Mommy to knock?"

She sighed. "Yes."

Eleanor knocked on the door and said, "I couldn't have reached the door if I was in Utah."

A muffled growl came from the other side of the door, "Come in!"

They entered the office and found Sergeant Leland Miller — a fifty-three-year-old Black man — sitting behind his desk eating a pack of peanut butter crackers.

"Sergeant Miller?" asked Vegas.

The sergeant looked at the two strange women and asked, "Who are you two? The Gilmore Girls?"

"I'm Vegas Chantly and I'm a private invest—" Vegas had to stop talking to get a better grip on the answering machine. "I'm a private investigator. Can I set this stupid machine down on your desk?"

"Looks like you better," the sergeant said as he watched her struggle.

Vegas sat the answering machine on the desk and let out a big sigh of relief like she was a whoopie cushion in action. She moved her arms back and forth to get some feeling into them and said, "Man, phone calls weighed more back then."

"I'm Eleanor Chantly," Eleanor said to the sergeant and offered her hand.

"Are you her client?" asked the sergeant.

"No. I'm her mom."

The sergeant looked at the two of them and said, "That makes sense — I guess." Then he stuck a cracker in his mouth and took a sip of coffee.

"Did you buy some new things or something?" Eleanor asked when she noticed a box of assorted items on the floor.

"I just got back from vacation, and I'm putting some stuff away," he replied.

"Where did you go?" asked Eleanor.

"Mom," interrupted Vegas, "that's not really any of our business."

"I don't mind. Seems like everybody wants to know what I do. I've been working this job for six years straight without any vacation, and I finally said, 'That's it, I'm taking a vacation.' I had it all planned out. I was going to go to Memphis for a blues convention, but the family had other plans. They wanted to go where the aliens crash-landed their flying saucer at Roswell, so that's where I went on my vacation, where all the crazy people live. And it looks like they followed me home," the sergeant said and stared at Vegas and Eleanor.

"I saw a UFO one time," Eleanor replied.

"Why am I not surprised," said the sergeant.

"I was out on the back porch when I saw it swoop down," Eleanor said while making a swooping motion with her hands.

"Mom, that wasn't a UFO, that was a bat," Vegas said.

"No it wasn't, it had wings. It also shot out a laser."

"Bats have wings. And it flew into the bug zapper. Don't you remember? The power blinked on and off for ten minutes afterward. We had to get a new TV."

"That was a coincidence."

"Meanwhile, back at the police department," the sergeant said, looking annoyed.

There was a knock at the door.

"Now what?" asked the sergeant in frustration. "Who is it?"

A voice on the other side shouted, "Sergeant Miller, sir!"

"I know who I am! Who are you?" the sergeant shouted in reply. This was not shaping up to be a good day.

"Officer Perkins, sir! Can I come in, sir?"

Sergeant Miller rubbed his face with a hand and said, "The room is kind of full of crazy people right now!"

Officer Cody Perkins, fresh from the academy, opened the door slightly and peeked his head inside. "I couldn't make out what you said," he stated. "Were you talking to me?"

"What do you want, Perkins?" Sergeant Miller asked.

Perkins entered the office, closed the door behind him, and said, "Sergeant, I was wondering if I could get another body camera."

"Another body camera?" queried the sergeant. "We just issued them this morning."

"What's a body camera?" Eleanor whispered to Vegas.

"Police officers wear them on their uniform to record their actions."

"It's like I'm your body camera," Eleanor said, and with a big smile, she laid her head on her daughter's shoulder. Vegas rolled her eyes.

"Did you break the camera or is it malfunctioning?" asked the sergeant.

"No, well, I ... I dropped it in the toilet, sir," Officer Perkins said.

There was a silence before the sergeant repeated what the young officer had just told him. "You dropped it in the toilet?"

"Yes, sir. It splashed and everything."

"That reminds me, I should have gotten some toilet paper when we were out this morning," Eleanor said.

"Not now, Mom."

The sergeant shot a look at the new officer. "If you were the one that dropped it in the toilet, then you're going to have to be the one to get it out."

"I can't do that, sir."

"Are you too precious or something?"

"No, it's—"

Before the officer could complete his thought the sergeant barked out, "Listen, you were the one that dropped it in there, so you have to be the one to fish it out. Understand?"

"But I can't do that, sir."

"I'm not going to do it for you. Do you understand that?" asked the sergeant.

"I understand that, sir. It's just ... well, I flushed it, sir."

There was a silence, combined with a "what did he just say" look from the other three.

"What do you mean that you flushed it?" Sergeant Miller asked slowly, drawing out the words.

"Handle down, sir."

"Why did you flush the toilet if your body camera was in it!" the sergeant practically screamed.

"Well, I was done, sir."

The sergeant threw up his hands in frustration.

"Did it go all the way through?" Eleanor asked.

"Yes, ma'am."

"That's some strong suction," she said.

"How in the world did the body camera go down the toilet?" the sergeant asked. "I know they're not tiny — we had to get the medium-sized ones for budget reasons."

"I did have to hold the handle down for a bit," Officer Perkins said.

"Why did you hold the handle down?" the now-frazzled sergeant asked.

"That's how it works, sir," replied the unflappable rookie.

Eleanor turned to Vegas and said, "We should tell the Rhinehouse Apartments janitor about these toilets. They're amazing."

The sergeant stood up, walked to the window, and looked out. He wasn't looking for anything in particular, he was just wondering if he could survive the jump.

Perkins then asked, "Sergeant, I need to know what I'm supposed to do."

"Just go away, Perkins, and I'll deal with you later," whispered the sergeant as he stared out the window at a rooftop billboard advertising a new reality show that was appropriately about septic tank builders.

"This won't come out of my paycheck will it, sir?" asked a concerned Officer Perkins.

"We'll see, Perkins."

"It's just that I already had to pay for that aardvark—"

"Leave, Perkins, just leave," the sergeant moaned. He closed his eyes as if hoping it would put a stop to this nightmare.

Officer Perkins reluctantly left.

Sergeant Miller then turned around, looked at Vegas and her mother, and asked, "What were we talking about?"

"Are you familiar with the Wilson Hopkins case?" Vegas asked. "He's the chess master who died the other day at the Rhinehouse Apartments."

"Yeah, I recall that. He hit his head or something when he was cleaning."

"Aha!" shouted Eleanor, which startled both the sergeant and Vegas.

"What is your problem?" Vegas asked.

"I thought it fit the moment," Eleanor said. "I was adding emphasis to the situation."

"You didn't add any emphasis," said Vegas, "you just added lunacy."

Sergeant Miller walked to his desk, stared down at the bulky answering machine, and asked, "What's with the hair dryer?"

Vegas plugged in the machine as she said, "This is the deceased's answering machine. I had to bring the whole thing because it's so old. It has a very interesting message on it that I want you to hear."

"I don't have time for this," the sergeant said in frustration.

"It won't take but a minute, I promise," Vegas said and pushed the play button. The answering machine message said, "Did you get those wieners?"

Vegas quickly turned off the machine. The sergeant stared at Vegas and asked, "Well, did you?"

"I went back too far. Just a second. Listen to the next message."

She hit play again, and this time it said, "I'm going to get you, chess man."

Eleanor shouted, "Aha!"

Vegas turned to her mother and said, "I have to admit, your emphasis did fit better that time."

"I'm learning," Eleanor said with a proud smile.

"When was that message recorded?" asked the sergeant.

"The day before his murder," Vegas said.

The sergeant observed, "If someone is going to kill somebody, why would they telegraph it on an answering machine?"

Eleanor asked, "Is that a joke? 'Telegraph it on an answering machine' — that's amusing."

"You know, Mom, most women your age have a hobby to keep them busy," Vegas said.

"You are my hobby," Eleanor said as she hugged Vegas and placed her head on her daughter's shoulder.

"The YMCA has a juggling class on Thursdays. Maybe you should try that out?" Vegas added.

"I can't juggle," Eleanor said, and then it hit her. "Oh — hence the class."

Vegas turned back to the sergeant and informed him, "We also found the janitor's hat in the victim's closet."

"*I* found it, actually," Eleanor said. "Being nosey finally paid off. Let that be a lesson to mothers everywhere."

"What hat?" asked the sergeant.

"The janitor's hat," Vegas said. "I think he might have been hiding in the closet, and when Hopkins' back was turned, he rushed out of the closet and attacked him, and in the chaos, he lost his hat."

"Was something stolen?" queried the sergeant.

"A trophy and a life," Vegas said.

"Why would someone steal a trophy?" the sergeant asked.

"Why would someone flush a body camera?" Vegas said. "People are weird."

The sergeant asked, "Are you sure it was the janitor's hat you found and not the victim's?"

"It is a very distinctive hat," Vegas said. "Everyone has seen him wearing it. The janitor's name is Billy Sanchez."

"You know, I once had a maintenance man come to my place to fix my dripping bathroom faucet, and he left his pants behind," Eleanor said.

"Mom! Inappropriate," Vegas said.

"Did the janitor have a motive to kill Hopkins?" asked the sergeant.

"I'm not sure," Vegas said. "Possibly. We talked to the

janitor earlier, and he said that Hopkins picked on him and bullied him for not playing chess."

"Why would he kill him over that?" the sergeant wondered.

"That's what investigations are for," reminded Vegas.

"Does the voice on the answering machine sound like the janitor?" asked the sergeant.

"I'm sure he disguised his voice," Vegas said. "Not all men talk like Batman."

The sergeant said, "I've got to be honest, I think you're finding something that isn't there. Now if you'll excuse me, I've got to make a sign that informs our officers to remove their body cameras when they go to the restroom."

"But—" Vegas said but was quickly cut off by the sergeant.

"We're done here. The door is that way." Sergeant Miller pointed at the door and began reading the papers on his desk.

Vegas picked up the answering machine and walked to the door with her mother following. But then Vegas stopped and turned back to the sergeant. "I think you're wrong, and I'm going to prove it," she said.

"And if we can't, we'll take it to the highest court in the land," Eleanor replied.

"That's not how it works, Mom."

"Never mind," Eleanor said.

They walked out the door and Eleanor slammed it shut behind them. "Oops!" She reopened the door and whispered, "I didn't mean to slam it." Then she shut the door quietly.

Vegas and her mother stood outside the sergeant's office.

"I can't believe that," Vegas said in an angry voice. "He didn't even take us seriously. Of course, you didn't really help."

"But we have evidence. A hat. A dead body. A missing trophy. A voice on an answering machine. I mean, the voice has to be from somebody, right? All we have to do is figure out who left it and why," Eleanor said.

"Billy Sanchez is the only suspect we have at the moment, but he doesn't seem to have a motive," Vegas said.

"His hat didn't get there by itself," Eleanor said.

"Someone could have put it there in an attempt to frame him for it."

"Do you think it was the sergeant?" Eleanor asked.

"Why on earth would Sergeant Miller try to frame a janitor?"

Eleanor thought it over and placed an index finger to her lips when an answer hit her. "So he wouldn't have to investigate the crime!"

"It would take longer to frame somebody than it would to investigate them."

"It's just a theory. So what do we do now?" asked Eleanor.

"You take me to the garage so I can get my vehicle, and then you can go home so I can work on this case by myself."

"But you need me."

"I need you to be safe, and private investigating is too dangerous for you to be a part of. I thank you for your help, but I can't concentrate on what I'm doing if I'm worried about you."

"But what are you going to do?" Eleanor asked.

"Maybe I'll do a stakeout."

"Oh, you're hungry, too. I'm craving hot dogs. I think it's because of the message on that machine about those wieners."

"I meant a stakeout of Billy Sanchez."

"Oh," Eleanor said. "Well, to be honest, that doesn't change anything for me. I'm still craving a hot dog."

Eleanor walked to her car as Vegas stood there momentarily and said to herself, "I might take her home and bury her in the leaves or something."

6

Eleanor and Vegas pulled into Bobby Dan's Garage on the outskirts of Blue Falls. Eleanor parked in front of a big plywood sign that was painted white with bold-red letters outlined in black that read, "Service with a Smile — if paying cash."

Vegas looked at the blue metal shop building with three garage bay doors all in the up position and saw a school of workers operating on various cars. She commented, "I have to admit that Bobby Dan does sound like a good name for a mechanic."

"Yeah. He seems to do good work. Your father always came to him."

Eleanor grabbed her purse and began to get out when Vegas grabbed her by the hand and said, "No, Mom. I want you to go home."

Eleanor was stunned by her daughter's suggestion. "Home? I can't go back home. I'm on a case."

"You're not on a case, Mom. I'm on a case. I'm the

private investigator. You're the crazy mom. Now you go back home and enjoy your retirement. That's the way life is supposed to work."

Vegas watched Eleanor's eyes fill with sadness as she said softly, "But I can't go home. There's nothing to do there."

"What about your TV game shows?" asked Vegas. "You're always talking about them. They have a whole cable network devoted to them now."

"I don't care about any game shows," Eleanor admitted sadly as she stared down at the steering wheel. "I only watch them out of boredom." Then she turned to her daughter with her eyes lit up and said, *This* is what I was meant to do. I've got the taste of danger in my mouth, Vegas, and I can't get it out."

Vegas stared at her mother a little concerned and said, "Danger in your mouth? That sounds disgusting."

"Well, what do you guys in the private investigator business call it?"

"A job."

They were quiet for a few seconds before Eleanor pleaded her case. "Let me stay with you for the rest of the day. Please. I'll not do anything bad or get in the way."

"Not do anything bad or get in the way?" Vegas asked in an unbelieving voice. "You're like a Coyote and Road Runner cartoon in which you play both characters. Now go home and relax. You've earned it."

"I can't relax if I'm worried about you. You need me to help you out with things."

"What kind of things?" Vegas asked.

"Driving you around. If I wasn't here, you wouldn't be here either. That's proof right there you need me to help you with things."

"I admit that I needed you to drive me today, and I really appreciate the help. But I'm here to get my vehicle so you don't have to drive me around anymore."

Vegas could see the disappointment on her mother's face. She knew that she didn't like being home alone, but she couldn't allow her to keep going out with her on cases, mainly for her own safety.

"I'll be fine," Vegas reassured her. "I understand why you feel this way, and I appreciate your concern. But this is what I do. I know how to take care of myself because you and Dad taught me how to."

Vegas could see that her mother was about to cry. She tried to console her by holding her hand.

"Listen, I know losing Dad earlier this year has been hard on you. It's been hard on both of us. But don't you see what you're doing? You're replacing Dad with me."

Tears streamed down Eleanor's face as she nodded and said, "I don't mean to get on your nerves or anything. It's just that I need to be with you in case something happens. The day your father died in the car accident, I was sleeping. Your father's routine had him getting up at six in the morning, and at six-thirty, he would go to Hardee's and get our breakfast. He'd get us a sausage and biscuit, some hash browns, and two cups of coffee. Then he would bring it back to me in the bedroom and we'd eat it together as the sun rose. That morning I overslept, and when I looked at the clock, it was past seven-thirty. I knew something was wrong."

Eleanor began to lose control of her emotions and Vegas put her hand on her mother's shoulder to try and reassure her.

"I didn't even get to tell him goodbye," Eleanor said sadly.

Vegas tried not to cry as they hugged.

"I know it's hard, but you have to live your life through you. Not me or Dad or anybody else. Dad wouldn't want you to be sad all the time."

"But I'm not sad when I'm with you," Eleanor balled.

Vegas smiled. "I understand, Mom. I do."

Vegas pulled away from her mother as Eleanor tried to compose herself. "I'm sorry," Eleanor said. "I didn't mean to cry like that."

"It's okay," replied Vegas. "You just need to establish a new routine, is all. You and Dad had a routine, and now you have to create one just for yourself."

"Maybe you're right."

Vegas had a thought. "Hey, remember a few weeks ago when you said you'd like to have a dog?"

"Yes," Eleanor nodded as she dried her eyes. "I had just watched a dog movie on the Hallmark Channel when I said that."

"But that's what you should do. There's a pet store down the street here. You can go there and see if you can find a dog or another pet. It'll be fun."

"But what if your car isn't ready? Don't I need to stay here until you find out for sure?"

"I'll call you if I need you."

"But you don't have a cellphone," Eleanor said.

"I'm sure the garage has a phone, Mom."

"Yeah. ... Oh, we still have that answering machine in the back here. You should take that back — hauling it around is ruining my gas mileage."

They both laughed.

"I'll do that. Now you go on and I'll call you later," Vegas said and kissed her mother on the cheek, then closed the vehicle door behind her.

As Vegas walked toward the garage, Eleanor got out of the vehicle and ran toward Vegas shouting, "Vegas!"

Vegas stopped and turned around and asked, "What is it?"

Eleanor hugged Vegas and said, "I love you."

"I love you too, Mom."

Eleanor ran back to her vehicle, got in, and slowly drove off.

Vegas shook her head and said, "Women."

"Can I help you?" asked a high-pitched Southern voice from behind her.

Vegas turned and found she was face to face with Bobby Dan, the garage owner. He probably weighed a little bit more than a large kitten and, like her, he stood all of five feet tall.

"I'm Vegas Chantly. I'm here about my vehicle."

"Sure, which one is it?" he asked as they both walked toward the garage.

"The Astro."

"Oh, yeah, I know which one you're talking about."

"Is it ready?"

"Ma'am, it'll never be ready."

Vegas stopped walking and looked at Bobby Dan with concern. "What do you mean it'll never be ready?"

"The frame is broken in three places, and one of the breaks is clean through. The engine is shot, and both axles are cracked. When we jacked it up, the left rear tire broke off and rolled into Bucky's leg."

"I hope Bucky is okay," Vegas said.

"Bucky's never been okay."

"So you need a couple more days?" Vegas asked in a joking tone.

"I'm afraid it would take a couple lifetimes to fix that vehicle, ma'am. I can't in good conscience allow you or anyone to ever drive that vehicle."

Vegas let out a big sigh. "That doesn't sound good."

"I can't believe you're not dead. You've been driving a coffin."

"I knew it was rattling a lot."

"It also had peanut butter on the battery terminal. Any idea how that got there?"

Vegas remembered her mother's credit card incident from earlier and responded, "Genetics."

Vegas wondered what in the world she was going to do. She had to have a car. She could borrow her mother's vehicle, but her mother would come with it. She had to get another car, she decided. And when she looked to her left, she saw it.

"What's that over there?" she asked.

"That is William Franks' seventy-nine red Pontiac Trans Am."

"I see a for sale sign on it."

"Yes, you do."

"Can I have a look at it?" she asked, not worrying about how she was actually going to pay for it.

"Yes, you can."

The two of them walked to the car. Vegas thought it was the most beautiful car she had ever seen. Her eyes ran over its body lines like a teenage boy staring at a pinup model. She even found her right hand stroking the side of it. She wasn't the best judge of cars, but this one was clean inside and out.

"It seems well taken care of," Vegas observed.

"It's peanut butter-free," Bobby Dan said.

"How many miles does it have?"

"Only forty-three thousand."

Vegas inspected the car and commented, "I don't see any rust."

"There's no rust. Mr. Franks has a large car collection and keeps them all housed in his garage. He has two full-time mechanics that keep them running in tip-top shape."

"Why is he selling this one?" Vegas asked as she pressed her nose against the passenger-side window with her hands on both sides of her face to see the interior better.

"His wife told him that he had to either choose the cars or her."

"And he chose her. That's kind of romantic," Vegas said with a smile as she straightened up from looking inside the vehicle.

"Not really. He chose the cars. She then got mad and shot him."

Vegas nodded and replied, "I understand his choice now. Is he okay?"

"Yeah. He can't sit down too well though. She shot him right in the butt."

"Was he running away or did the night just get really awkward?" Vegas asked.

"I don't know about that part. All I know is that he's selling the car to help pay his medical bills."

"Is he staying with his wife?"

"Has to, I guess. Hey, she shot him, so she should have to change the bandages."

"That's true. How much does he want for it?"

"Thirty-one thousand."

Vegas stared at the car longingly. She didn't have that much money. But neither did she have a vehicle of any kind, and she had to have a vehicle.

"I've always liked these Firebirds," Vegas said. "I like the T-Tops best."

"Well, this one has a T-Top. They got big when the *Smokey and the Bandit* movie came out a long time ago. You'd see them all over town. I guess that was a little bit before your time, though."

"I've seen *Smokey and the Bandit.* I liked the car on *The Rockford Files,* too. I watched the reruns when I was a little girl and loved the car. I also had a thing for Jim Rockford. And Burt Reynolds. I wasn't as picky for boyfriends when I was eight."

He nodded disinterestedly. "So you want it?"

Vegas found herself going over every conceivable option, but none seemed great. Maybe she could get it on some type of installment plan. She knew car sellers usually wanted all cash up front so they didn't have to deal with payments, but this might be her only hope.

"I'll have to think about it. Has anyone else made you an offer on it yet?"

"I've had several people look at it, but no one has made me an offer."

"Will he only consider thirty-one thousand?" Vegas queried.

"Everything is negotiable."

"Maybe I should just marry him," Vegas said as she walked around the car and opened the door, and looked in.

Bobby Dan laughed. "You'd probably have to promise not to shoot him in the butt before he'd agree to marry you."

"I'm not signing any prenuptial agreement. I got my pride."

Vegas looked at the car some more. She wanted it. She had always dreamed about this car. Now here she was standing beside it!

But she couldn't afford it.

"You know," Bobby Dan said, recognizing he almost had the sale locked up, "he's willing to do a payment plan."

Vegas cocked her head and smiled.

7

E leanor opened the glass door and walked into Little Critter's Pet Shop. A little bell on the door announced her arrival with a little ding-a-ling.

The owner of the shop was an attractive Asian woman in her thirties who was sitting behind a counter to the right of the front entrance. She greeted Eleanor with a smile and said, "Can I help you?"

"I just wanted to look around for a minute," Eleanor replied as she gave a gentle back-and-forth wave of her hand.

"Okay. If you need any help with anything, just let me know," the pet shop owner said with a tight-lipped smile.

"I will. Thank you."

The pet shop's phone rang and the owner picked it up as Eleanor began walking around the shop. The store was surprisingly clean, she thought. The animals were cordoned in attractive displays, the endless choices of food and supplies were stacked neatly on shelves in beautiful packaging, and even the poop scoopers looked nice.

She spotted something in a cage with a long tail that gave her an uneasy feeling. She had no idea what it was. To her, it looked like a cross between a squirrel and a mop with half of its handle missing.

Eleanor continued to walk slowly around the shop and eventually stopped in front of a fish tank to watch the fish swim about.

"I could never be a goldfish," she said aloud to herself. "I just can't stand to eat wet food. Or fit into the tank," she added with a laugh.

She walked around some more and came upon a beautiful parrot. It was a large bird and overwhelmed her with its sheer size. She had seen parrots on TV, of course, but never in person. How pirates carried them around on their shoulders was an amazing feat, she thought. And maybe that explained the eye patch so many pirates wore.

"Can I help you?"

Eleanor stared at the bird, fascinated that it could talk so clearly.

"I'm just looking around," Eleanor said. "It's amazing how well you can talk."

"No, I'm over here."

Eleanor turned and saw the pet shop owner.

"Can I help you?" she asked again, which made Eleanor laugh.

"Oh, I thought the bird was talking," Eleanor replied as a hint of redness filled her face. "I feel so dumb right now."

"It's nothing to be embarrassed about. This is Oscar. He was rescued from a place that had over fifty parrots."

"Fifty?" Eleanor said. "I didn't know it was possible to take care of that many of anything."

"It wasn't. The owner sort of got lost in their world and didn't think of the world they were creating for the birds."

Eleanor was taken aback by the words of wisdom. Was that what she was doing with Vegas?

"Are you interested in a parrot?" the pet shop owner asked.

"No, I don't think so. I'm fascinated by them. I mean, having a pet that can talk is amazing, but I would worry it would backfire on me. He'd end up telling people what I said during the day, and to be honest, my words aren't always Christian. I probably wouldn't have a friend left in the world then," Eleanor said and laughed.

"I understand," the shop owner said with a hint of amusement in her eyes. "We have—"

But she could suggest another pet, Eleanor asked, "How would you cook one of these things?"

"Cook? You mean cook a parrot?" the pet shop owner asked in horror.

"Well, I mean I wouldn't buy it to cook. I wouldn't do anything like that unless it bit me or something."

There was an uneasy silence between the two of them for a few seconds before the pet shop owner said, "Are you looking for a pet or something to eat?"

Eleanor sensed she may have offended the owner and tried to calm things down.

"I was just kidding. I wouldn't, you know, actually do that. You know, eat my pet."

Again there were several moments of silence, filled this time by actual cricket chirping, courtesy of the feeder crickets.

Eleanor tried to change the subject from dinner to her purpose of being there as she said, "To be honest, I don't know what I'm looking for. See, my husband passed away earlier this year, and I've been hanging around with my daughter a lot, and it appears that I'm getting on her nerves."

"I can understand that," said the pet shop owner. Eleanor frowned. This conversation was not going well.

"Well, I don't see that at all myself, but life is as life is, I guess," countered Eleanor. "So I thought if I had a companion of some kind to hang around with me at home, I wouldn't be bugging my daughter so much."

Eleanor noticed a pretty fish in a tank in front of her.

"Oh, that's an interesting fish. What kind is it?"

"That's a puffer fish," the pet shop owner informed her as they admired it.

"It's beautiful," Eleanor said.

"They are beautiful fish. People like them because they bring some excitement to their life."

"A fish brings excitement?" asked an unbelieving Eleanor.

"Yes. See, the puffer fish is poisonous."

"Poisonous?" exclaimed Eleanor. "Why would anyone want a poisonous fish?"

"Some people like the danger."

Eleanor stared at the puffer fish for a moment and then turned and scanned the store.

"Well, you appear to have quite an array of animals here — birds that talk, fish that can kill you. But do you have any animals here that won't fill my life with fear if I took them home?" Eleanor asked in a concerned voice.

"Would you be interested in a cat or dog?"

"I'm not a cat person. Do you have any chickens? I had one when I was little."

"Is this to eat?" asked the pet shop owner.

"Oh, no. I wouldn't eat it if I had it as a pet."

"I'm afraid that we don't have any chickens. We have rabbits."

"Rabbits? They don't seem like they would be much of a companion. They just sort of sit there, don't they? Be like being married again," Eleanor said with a hearty laugh.

"Well, they're pretty to look at," the pet shop owner said in an attempt to make a sale.

"That's what my mirror is for," Eleanor said with a laugh, but again the shop owner didn't join her in laughing. She didn't seem to get jokes, Eleanor thought.

"We have a ferret, if you're interested in that," the owner suggested as she approached a cage.

Eleanor looked at the ferret in the cage and observed, "I don't know. It seems a little rat-like to me."

"There are a lot of people that have ferrets and even take them to shows similar to that of dog shows. They are becoming very popular."

"I think I'll pass on the ferret."

"How about some goldfish then?"

"I did see them when I came in. Of course, I'd have to buy a tank and all the supplies that would go with it, which is a lot of money. Then you have to change the water and everything. Fish are just too boring for me to go through that much trouble. I mean, what can you do with a fish? You can't take one out and play with it except to throw it up and let it splash back down into the tank. Not that I would do that," Eleanor quickly added.

"I see," the pet shop owner said in a tone that suggested she hoped Eleanor would just leave.

"Maybe if I looked around just a little bit more, something would—"

Then Eleanor looked to her right and saw a basset hound. She cocked her head and smiled.

8

Vegas stood in front of her camper washing her brand-new purchase, the red seventy-nine Pontiac Trans Am. She was proud of her negotiating skills, which had resulted in only five thousand dollars down and a manageable monthly payment. As long as she didn't have any financial emergencies, she should be able to meet the payments with a little room to spare.

It was the first car she had purchased herself. The minivan, like the camper she lived in, belonged to her parents. She felt like she had reached a turning point in her life. She was a grownup now, a woman on the move. A full-fledged adult who lived in a camper park in a silver Airstream with Woody Woodpecker painted on the side. Hey, she thought, everybody grows up in their own way at their own speed, and there was nothing wrong with that.

At that moment Eleanor arrived. She was surprised to see her daughter washing a car.

"Are you starting a car-washing business now?" Eleanor

asked as she got out of her SUV and looked the Trans Am up and down. "I would have let you wash mine first so you could get a handle on how to do it."

"What is there to washing a car?" Vegas asked and then accidentally stepped in her wash bucket and turned it over. "Ah, man," she groaned.

"What is there to playing chess? But that may have got somebody murdered," reminded her mother.

"I suppose you have a point," Vegas said as she turned her bucket right side up. "But I'm not washing this car for money. This baby's mine."

Vegas placed one hand on her hip and twirled her other hand like a game show model.

"Yours? So this is my first grandchild?" Eleanor asked in an unbelieving voice.

"You can look at it however you want," Vegas said with a smile. "I think I'll call him Thor."

"Thor? I thought everyone named their cars after girls."

"Not me. I'm riding Thor. That has a nice ring to it."

"But how in the world can you afford a car like this?" Eleanor asked.

"Bobby Dan worked it out for me. Just made a down payment, and the rest I pay monthly. Then within a few years, she's all mine. Forever."

"How much was it?"

"A lady doesn't say how much she spends on her new love," Vegas said in a bad British accent.

Eleanor walked around the car and looked impressed. "I have to say, this is nice. Your father would have loved to have had a car like this. He was always into fast cars, but he could never afford one. Well, he said he couldn't afford one, but I think he thought it was wrong for him to spend that much money on something just for himself."

"Go ahead and get in," said Vegas, which didn't take much persuasion, as Eleanor quickly opened the door and plopped down into the driver's seat.

"Dad's the one that gave me my taste in cars. There's not a spot of rust on it either. It was owned by some big shot. He has a whole collection of cars. Has mechanics that take care of them and everything."

"How come he sold this one?" Eleanor asked.

"Uh, I don't know," Vegas said. She did *not* want to tell her mom about the buttocks shooting — that would only spark a wild conversation and a rebuke for buying a car from such a person.

"It looks like a private investigator's car, all right," Eleanor said as she ran her hands over the steering wheel. She got out, closed the door, and asked, "Does it run better than the minivan?"

"You run better than the minivan, Mom."

"Speaking of the minivan, where is it?"

Vegas was hesitant to answer the query but realized she had to tell her the truth. She sighed and summed it up in one word: "Buried."

"What do you mean buried? Did you wreck it?"

"No, I didn't wreck it this time," Vegas assured her. "They took it to the car crusher."

"But that was still my vehicle. I only loaned it to you because I got the SUV. Why would you let them crush it?"

"It was a total loss. It couldn't be fixed."

"That's the oldest scam in the book," Eleanor said with her hands on her hips as she slipped into her mother-knows-best mode. "They tell you your car is trash and then they sell you another car you can't afford."

"The car was trash. And this car I can afford. Eventually, you know, over time," Vegas said as she finished washing the car with her big yellow sponge.

"You'll need to get a lot of cases to pay this off."

"I have a case, remember? And I've been thinking about it as I washed my car. It's very therapeutic to wash your car — it lets your mind wander and puts things into perspective."

"I know exactly what you mean because I've been doing some thinking, too. Let me show you what I got."

"Oh, no," Vegas mumbled.

Eleanor went to her vehicle, opened the back door, and scooped up the basset hound she purchased from the pet shop. She carried him with her arms wrapped under his front legs, showing him belly side out, and grinned from ear to ear as she approached Vegas.

"Ta-da!" Eleanor said as she struggled to hold the dog. "Our problems are over."

"Our problems will never be over," Vegas corrected her.

"I mean our problems in fighting crime. ... Man, he weighs a lot for a short dog," Eleanor said.

"I don't think we should be throwing dogs at people, Mom."

"No, we're not going to throw him at anybody. That's not what I meant. He's not a boomerang."

"Look, you bought a dog, good for you. Now you have someone else to play with during the day instead of me."

"No, it's for us," Eleanor said and tried to hold the dog up for her daughter to admire.

"What do you mean for us? I bought my own toy today. I don't need yours."

"He'll help us on the case."

"I don't—" Vegas stopped her thought so as to offer a helpful suggestion: "You might want to put him down before you throw your back out."

"That's a good idea," Eleanor said and set the dog on the ground. "I call him Buttermilk."

"Buttermilk?"

"I thought it fit," Eleanor said as the dog lay on the ground and closed its eyes as if it was in desperate need of sleep.

"He seems to have the consistency of buttermilk," Vegas said. "What's the leash for?"

"So he won't run away."

Vegas looked at the sleeping dog and observed, "I don't think you're going to have a problem with that. Now, how in the world is he going to help us on the case?"

"He's a sniffing dog. He also drools a little more than I expected, but I'll train him."

"Well, first of all, all dogs are sniffing dogs, Mom."

"I mean a tracker. He can smell something and then follow the trail and lead us to the killer. I've seen it on a million detective shows."

"What's he going to smell to help him find the bad guy?" Vegas asked.

"The hat I found in the closet."

"We already know who owns the hat. It belongs to the janitor. Remember?"

Eleanor thought for a moment and said, "Then maybe the answering machine. He could smell it and tell us who it belongs to."

"We already know who owns the answering machine."

Eleanor tried again to think of a job for the basset hound and came up with, "He can listen to the voice on the answering machine and then follow it to the person who said it."

"That doesn't sound like any detective shows I've ever heard of. It sounds more like something that would happen in a cartoon. Do you want to wash him before I throw my water out?"

"Nah. He's pretty clean. For a dog anyway."

"How much was he?" asked Vegas.

"I paid three hundred dollars for him. Surely he can track something."

"Three hundred dollars?" Vegas replied as she shook her head and rolled her eyes, then picked up the bucket of water and dumped it behind her camper. "I think he should move a little more for that much money." She began winding up the garden hose in her arms.

"We're still learning about each other right now. I'm sure he's more active at different times of the day. What are you going to do now?" asked Eleanor.

"I'm going to go back to the apartment."

"Why?" Eleanor asked as she petted her new dog.

CHECKMATE A KILLER   77

"I have my reasons," Vegas said as she placed the water hose beneath the Airstream along with the empty bucket.

"I'll come with you and bring Buttermilk! This will be his first real test at solving crimes."

"No, Mom. I don't need you to come with me. I've got a car now. You can go and play with Buttermilk at home or take him to the park and watch him sleep in front of the other dogs."

"I'd rather watch you. You're very fascinating sometimes. I think Buttermilk would enjoy watching you, too."

"Yeah, boy."

"What are you going to do at the apartment building?" Eleanor asked.

"I got to thinking while I was washing my car: Maybe there's a security camera there. If so, then that might help clear up a few things."

"Are you leaning one way or the other on what happened? Do you think Sanchez did it?"

"The hat in the closet seems too convenient. Also, I have no idea why Sanchez would want to kill Wilson."

"Maybe they were fighting over a girl."

Vegas went to her car and opened the door.

"Aren't you going to let me go with you?" asked a sad-faced Eleanor.

"No, Mom. We've already had this conversation. The mom goes home and the daughter goes to work. It's the way it is all around the world."

"Did you want to take Buttermilk to help you?"

Vegas looked at Buttermilk sound asleep on the ground.

"I don't really want to wake him up. He seems tired. Now, you go on home, and I'll call you when I get back."

"Okay. You be careful now. There are crazy people out there that would take advantage of a pretty girl."

"I'll be fine. Love you."

"I love you more."

"That's probably true," mumbled Vegas.

"Dog-gone right!" Eleanor said and watched Vegas drive out of the park and head toward the Rhinehouse Apartments.

Eleanor walked to Buttermilk and sat on the ground beside him.

"Well, Buttermilk, it's just you and me now. Two old dogs with nothing to do. I have to admit, I'm worried about Vegas. She's in a profession that involves murder, for crying out loud. Why couldn't she have done something else that was less worrisome for a mother? She took typing in high school. She could have done something with that. She also took home economics, and as you can tell from this place, she failed that class. It seems like I'm always trying to save her from something or other."

Eleanor looked at the silver Airstream with the Woody Woodpecker painted on the side and shook her head. "Where did I go wrong with that little girl? I mean, who lives in a camper park? I mean besides Yogi Bear."

Eleanor sighed as she looked down at her sleeping friend and said, "I wish I could sleep like you. You don't seem to have any worries. Of course, you probably don't have a daughter. Moms worry about their daughters. It's what we do best."

Eleanor thought for a bit and then said, "I'm not going to let her do this alone. I'd be a poor mother for not protecting my baby. Come on, Buttermilk. To the Batmobile! We've got a case to solve and a daughter to save."

She scooped up Buttermilk in her arms, put him in the vehicle, and drove off to save her daughter.

9

V egas pulled into the Rhinehouse Apartments complex in her flashy new ride at one in the afternoon. She got out of her car, gave it a little pat on the top with a smile, then stood beside it looking at the front entrance of the building. Vegas spotted a security camera over the front portico; anybody that went in or out of the building's front entryway would be recorded.

She walked to the sidewalk that wrapped around the complex and headed east. At the corner, she spotted another security camera. Next, she walked to the corner of the building where a wood fence stood. She looked between the slats of the fence and saw two large green trash bins in the back parking lot, in which stood a white-painted sign that said "Private Use."

Vegas then went back to the sidewalk, turned west, and went to the corner. There she saw another security camera.

"This has to be the most secure bad-looking apartment building in all of Blue Falls," she said.

Vegas walked around the building to an alley that led to the back street. It was lined with pine trees on both sides, and large holes peppered the pavement, which made it look like the surface of the moon.

As she walked down the alley, she found a gate with a sign painted on it that said: Tenants Parking Only. She lifted the gate latch, opened the door, and proceeded to walk to the center of the parking lot. On the back of the building were rows of balconies that were attached to each apartment. It looked more like the kind of cheap motel that littered the outskirts of every city in the US than an apartment building.

When Vegas turned to go back to the front, a man in a uniform approached her. "Who are you?" he asked angrily.

"I'm me. Who are you?" Vegas asked.

"Don't get smart with me, lady. You're trespassing. What are you doing here?"

"I'm looking for some information."

"Like what?" he asked.

"Are you the security officer here?"

"Yes, ma'am. I'm Jim Bob Cooter."

The name caught her by surprise and she tried to suppress a giggle. Was that really his name? It sounded made up, she thought.

The security guard wore a dark-blue uniform. It was tight in the belly region, which made Vegas think this guy wasn't one to work out. His hat also seemed a bit tight, as if he was an extra in a Benny Hill sketch.

"Now tell me who you are," Jim Bob Cooter said in what he apparently thought was a menacing voice.

"I'm Vegas Chantly. I'm a private investigator."

"I don't care who you are," he replied.

"You just asked me who I was," Vegas said. She was getting a vibe that the guy thought he was quite important.

The security guard brushed off the slip-up and asked, "What are you investigating?"

"Bosco Hopkins hired me to investigate the death of his brother, Wilson. Do you know anything about that?"

The security guard's demeanor changed. His tough-guy facade melted, and he had the look of a little boy caught doing something he wasn't supposed to be doing with the dog. He seemed to be taken aback and wasn't clear on what he should say or do.

"Uh, yes," he said clumsily. "I was the one that called the police."

"You called the police?" Vegas asked. Interesting, she thought — Bosco had said he called them.

"Yes. I heard screaming and went to check it out."

"Screaming? Who was screaming?"

"When I went to the apartment, I saw Bosco screaming."

"He was outside his brother's apartment?"

"Yes. He had just found him. I went inside and saw Wilson lying on the floor. It was terrible," the security guard said.

"Could you tell what his injury was?"

"No. He was just lying on the floor."

"Face up or down?"

"I don't remember."

"You don't remember?"

The guard's eyes and facial expressions contorted. Vegas knew something wasn't right here.

"I tried to block that out. I've never seen a dead body before."

"What did you do after you saw the body?"

"I went out and told Bosco that I would call nine-one-one. Then about ten minutes later, the police came, and an ambulance was right behind them."

Vegas examined his pudgy white face as he talked. She was sure he was hiding information. How could he not remember if the body was face up or face down? That bothered her. If it was the first time he had ever seen a dead body, it seemed that it would have been etched into his mind. And why was he saying he called the police when Bosco said he did? Was one of them just remembering it wrong? Did it even matter?

"Did the police have any doubt that it was an accident?" Vegas asked.

"No, they pretty much thought that from the beginning, but Bosco wouldn't have any of it. He said his brother was murdered and he was going to prove it. I guess that's when he called you."

"Did the police interview any of the neighbors?"

"Not that I know of."

"Did you ask around to see if anybody heard anything or if they saw anybody suspicious hanging around?"

"There was no need to, it was an accident," the security officer said.

"You have to be sure," Vegas said in a scolding tone. "You could have asked to see if anyone heard him fall. That would have taken all of one minute. And we would have known when it happened."

"Well, I didn't see any need for that."

The two of them stared at each other, neither seeming to trust the other.

"I see that you have security cameras up," Vegas observed.

The security officer looked toward the building. He seemed lost all of the sudden, like he had forgotten where he was. After a moment he said, "Yes. We have them on the corners over the entrance and one in each hallway."

"You have them in the hallways?"

"Yes."

"Did the police notice this?"

"I guess not."

"Are they hidden from view?"

"No. They're just there."

"Did you tell the police about the security cameras?"

"No. Why are you asking all of these questions?"

"It's my job. Supposed to be yours, too."

The security officer became upset. "I don't need you telling me how to do my job, lady."

"I'd like to take a look at them," Vegas said.

"At what?"

He knew what she was talking about, Vegas thought. Was he attempting to stall for time while he came up with a suitable answer?

"The security footage. That's what we were just talking

about. Remember?" Vegas replied in a calm, confident manner.

"Why do you want to look at that?"

"To see if someone killed Wilson Hopkins."

The security officer looked like he didn't know what to do. He looked away from Vegas and toward the building, then glanced back at her.

"You're looking at the building like it's going to run away or something," Vegas said.

"I can't just let anyone look at the security cameras. You would have to get permission from the building owner."

"Someone may have been killed in this apartment building. You are the security officer here. I would think—"

"Are you blaming me for this?" he interrupted angrily.

"I'm not blaming anyone. I'm not even sure someone was killed here. It could have just been an accident like the police said. But having footage from the hallway and outside the building will go a long way toward figuring out exactly what happened."

"I can't show it to you unless you get permission from the owner of the building. Sorry."

"Did you do your rounds that night?"

"Rounds? Sure. I walk around every now and then to see if everything is okay."

"You could just use the security camera monitors for that. Save you the time of walking," Vegas said.

"I don't have to answer your questions, lady. You're not the police. In fact, you're trespassing."

"I was invited here by one of the tenants to investigate a possible murder. That's not trespassing."

"It is to me. I'm going to have to ask you to leave."

The security guard stood his ground and placed his right hand on his gun in an attempt to scare off Vegas.

"Well, who owns the building?" she asked.

"None of your business."

Vegas stayed calm. "Why are you making this so difficult? All I want is some information that could clear things up, and all you're doing is trying to make that impossible. Now, why is that?"

"I believe I told you to leave."

"I believe I asked you who owned the building. You can tell me or I can go to the cops and have them come back out here and ask you. And while they're here, they can have a look at your security cameras and check your credentials to make sure you didn't lie on your resume to get this job."

The security guard froze. "You don't know what you're talking about," he mumbled.

"Listen, it looks like we've got off on the wrong foot here. Why don't we just go to your office and call the owner for permission to look at the security footage?"

"No."

Vegas now began to wonder just how much he was hiding. This wasn't making sense.

"Why not?"

He didn't reply and started walking away before he abruptly stopped and turned and yelled, "You need to leave the premises, now!"

Vegas watched him disappear around the building. She

tried to make sense of the frustrating conversation, but her thoughts were interrupted by a barking dog.

Vegas turned her head toward the sound of the barking and saw a person near the corner of the building. She hoped it was a resident who could provide her with some answers.

When she got to the corner of the building, she saw her mother pressed up hard against the trash bin, as if she was trying to be invisible. Buttermilk had wrapped his leash around Eleanor's legs and was barking. Probably because he couldn't get away from this odd little woman either, Vegas thought.

"Mom, what are you doing here?"

"Shoot, you saw me," Eleanor said in disgust.

"I actually heard Buttermilk first."

"I didn't even know he could bark. Say, could you get him unwrapped from around my legs?"

Vegas shook her head and unclipped the leash from Buttermilk, then untangled the leash from her mother's legs. She clipped the leash back on Buttermilk's collar and addressed her mom. "Why are you here?"

"I was investigating," Eleanor replied as she straightened out her clothes.

"I think you might want to refine your investigating skills then, because you're not supposed to draw attention to yourself. Now, I need to go find out who owns this apartment building. You need to stay away from me."

"Let me help. You won't even know we're around."

"The whole world knows when you're around, Mom," Vegas said as she walked away.

"Honey, come back!"

"Why?" Vegas shouted.

"My blouse is hung up on the bin! And I stepped in something that I'm praying is chewing gum!"

Vegas didn't reply.

"Honey?" Eleanor said. "Honey?"

10

The drive to the Blue Falls Courthouse only took ten minutes, but Vegas, still annoyed at her mother, used that time to enjoy her new car. She opened up the throttle on the highway, letting the roar of the engine intoxicate her. The car's sportiness, its color, and its muscle-car engine seemed to match her personality perfectly. And people noticed — with the T-tops off, the car and its driver seemed to catch the eye of just about everyone she passed.

She got to the courthouse parking lot and was surprised by the abundance of parking spaces. Vegas thought the car was bringing her good luck, because finding a parking space at the courthouse was usually impossible at this time of day.

However, her excitement quickly turned to depression when she got to the courthouse front entrance. There she was met with a locked door that had a piece of yellow paper taped to it. It read, "Closed for the day because of water leak in ceiling. People upstairs in building inspector's office are idiots." It also had a little frown face in the lower right corner.

Vegas couldn't believe her luck. And then she ran into her mother again.

As she turned to head back to her car, she was startled to find herself facing her mother. "Ah! Why are you always scaring me to death, Mom?" she said as she placed her hand over her heart.

"I didn't mean to scare you. I was just following you, which is pretty easy to do in that red Camaro of yours."

"It's not a Camaro, it's a Trans Am. Like Burt Reynolds drove. Now, why are you following me?"

"To see where you were going. I thought that's self-explanatory."

"And why do you need to know that?"

"I don't know, I just worry about you during the day, is all. Worrying is what I do best. Well, that and wolfing down a box of Nilla Wafers. I just love those things."

"Well, you found me. You can go home now."

Eleanor looked in the parking lot and pointed out a blue Corvette.

"Your father had a car like that. I think it was green, though. Remember?"

"That's a Corvette. Dad had a Jeep Cherokee."

A sour expression splashed across Eleanor's face as she tried to line up her memory with the correct vehicle. "Well anyway, it drove well. Why don't men ask for directions when they drive?"

Vegas stared at her mother and asked, "What does that have to do with anything?"

"It just popped into my head. The other day I had the theme song to *Curb Your Enthusiasm* in my head, and I have no reason why. So why do you think that men don't ask for directions?"

"Because they're in it for the gas mileage. As long as they get twenty miles to the gallon, they don't care where they end up."

Eleanor thought that over. "I've never heard it explained like that before. It makes sense when you think about it. Hey, maybe you should write a book about men. You could call it, 'Men: All You Never Wanted to Know.'
"

Vegas felt herself becoming exasperated and asked, "Why aren't you home feeding Buttermilk?"

Eleanor bent down and rubbed Buttermilk's face. "He ate enough today, didn't you, buddy? But more importantly, why are you at the courthouse? Did you already get a speeding ticket?"

"No, I came here to look up who owned the Rhinehouse Apartments building. The security guard refused to tell me."

"Why wouldn't he tell you?"

"I don't know. It's a little suspicious to me. He wouldn't show me the security video either."

"Maybe they don't have a security camera," Eleanor said.

"I saw three on the building, and he mentioned that they have them in the hallways as well. That answer to the whole case could be on those cameras, and some guy named Jim Bob Cooter wouldn't let me see anything."

"They have security cameras on the side of the building?" asked Eleanor.

"Yeah. Why?"

Eleanor seemed embarrassed and didn't reply.

"Why, Mom?" Vegas repeated.

"I, well, I had to go to the bathroom when I was there earlier."

Vegas looked at her mother with a shocked expression on her face. "Mom! You went to the bathroom outside?"

"Well, it's too late to deny it since I'm on film," Eleanor said as she threw her arms up in the air. "I'm going to end up on one of those funny home video shows, ain't I? Before they go to a commercial about copper skillets, they'll say to stay tuned to see the fat lady go to the bathroom beside a trash bin."

Vegas shook her head and closed her eyes and asked, "Why didn't you go inside the building and see if they had a public restroom? Or go to one of the stores in the area?"

"When a girl's gotta go, she's gotta go. I heard it's not healthy for you to hold it too long because it might cause one of your pipes to burst. Plus, you're not thinking straight when you have to go that bad."

Eleanor shook her head. "I wish I was dead. Or at least had a bigger bladder. I'm so sorry, honey. Mommy will never do that again."

Vegas didn't say anything, so Eleanor asked in a distressed voice, "Am I still allowed to be your mother?"

"Yes," Vegas said with a sigh. "If I got rid of you every time you embarrassed me, you'd have been gone a long time ago."

"Thank you," Eleanor said in relief as she hugged her daughter.

"You can let go, Mom. People are staring."

Eleanor let go and straightened her daughter's clothes where the hug had rumpled them.

"I guess I'll go on back home then since, well, since I've embarrassed my beautiful child."

Eleanor started to walk away with Buttermilk when Vegas called out, "Mom!"

Eleanor quickly turned and rushed to Vegas' side.

"What is it, honey? I'll do whatever you want. I don't want to go home because there's nothing on TV right now."

"Now, I'm going to say something, and I don't want you to get too excited."

Her statement filled Eleanor with curiosity, and she replied, "That's interesting. I don't think you've ever told me that before. What is it?"

"I need you to take me to Pepper's house."

"You need me?" Eleanor asked in a happy voice. She kneeled down in front of Buttermilk and rubbed the sides of his head and said, "Our baby needs us! See, I told you following her wasn't morally wrong. Okay, Vegas, what do — You're going to have to help me back up."

Vegas gave her a hand and said, "Pepper lives in the mountains, and I don't want to take my car."

"Are you afraid that Smokey and the Bandit would get mad at you or something?"

"I need a four-wheel-drive."

"How come you didn't just ask to borrow it?"

Vegas twisted her mouth and closed her eyes and said, "You'll see. Let's go."

She began to walk away but suddenly stopped and turned back to her mother. "Uh, Mom."

"What is it, honey?"

"Do you need to go to the bathroom before we go?"

"No, I'm good. To be honest, I don't think I'll need to go again for three days after today."

E leanor's passengers were resting as she drove the mountain road. Buttermilk was sleeping in the back seat, and Vegas sat in the front passenger seat with her eyes closed. She was pondering the Hopkins case, trying to put all the information in some semblance of order.

Eleanor was enjoying the drive. There were beautiful bright-green trees all around, the sun was warm and inviting, and the sounds of birds added a lovely musical score to the day.

Eventually, Eleanor noticed there weren't any other vehicles on the road. She thought that was odd, being that it was so beautiful up there. Before she could make the observation to her daughter, she looked ahead and noticed there was no more road. It just suddenly stopped at the edge of a forest, with no hint of being able to go any further in a car or even on foot.

"What happened to the road?" Eleanor asked as she stopped the SUV in front of some small bushes.

Vegas opened her eyes and simply said, "It becomes a little tougher now is all."

"A little tougher now? It looks a little impossible now," exclaimed Eleanor. "What am I supposed to do?"

"Just drive on," ordered Vegas.

"There is no 'just drive on.' The road stops here," Eleanor said.

"It doesn't stop here. Pepper just lets all the bushes grow up to hide the road, is all. Once you drive through here, you'll see the road again, and then you just drive up it."

Eleanor looked at her daughter, and then at the bushes in front of her SUV. "Are you sure about this?"

"Yeah. I've been up here before," Vegas said.

"You came up here in the minivan?"

"Yeah."

Eleanor stared at the impossible woods ahead of her and said, "I'm guessing that's why the minivan died."

"I'm sure it didn't help. But we'll be fine. You're in a four-wheel-drive, so it should go a lot smoother."

Eleanor stared at the unseen path ahead of her and whispered, "I'm not sure about this."

"Just put it in four high so we can get up to his house," Vegas said.

"Why can't you just call him?"

"He'll only do favors if you visit him. And besides, he doesn't have a phone. He thinks phones are part of a government conspiracy."

Eleanor gave Vegas a "so he's a nut" look.

"It sounds worse than it is," said Vegas. Then, seeing that her mother was still hesitant to drive, she commanded, "Just go forward."

Eleanor pulled her SUV up to the shrubs, trusting that her daughter knew what she was talking about. She slowly pushed through the shrubs. The SUV's tires drove over rocks and stumps for a moment, and then she spotted the road.

Well, "road" might have overstated what it actually was. It consisted mostly of small gullies that were formed by rainwater and large rocks as they plummeted down the mountainside. The path was about eight feet wide, with trees pushing in on the sides. It appeared to meander up toward the treetops.

"I'm supposed to go up that?" Eleanor asked.

"That's why I wanted you to come along. It takes two people to navigate."

"Maybe you should drive," Eleanor said as she stared at the rough road ahead of her.

"I need to get out every now and then and move rocks and stuff. Nothing personal, but I'm a little stronger than you."

Eleanor looked like she was about to walk into a haunted house. "I have to admit I'm terrified right now."

"You'll do fine, Mom."

Eleanor just gripped the steering wheel as hard as she could and tried to work up the courage to journey up the perilous road.

"Do you want me to drive?" asked Vegas.

Eleanor thought it over for a few seconds and said, "No. I'm going to see it through. I guess this is what being a private investigator is these days. Maybe instead of buying that little red car of yours, you should have gotten one of those monster trucks."

Eleanor slowly pushed on the gas pedal and little by little made her way up the hill. Every now and then Vegas got out to move rocks or branches that had washed into the path. She also had to guide her mother over some small gullies, trying to hit them at angles so only one tire would be in the hole at a time, so as to limit the possibility of getting stuck. Slowly they made their way up the two-mile path until it flattened out and they came upon a house.

Like the road that wasn't a road, the house wasn't really a house. It would be better described as a shack, or perhaps a large garbage bin.

It was about twelve feet wide by twelve feet long, and the front door — which appeared to have come off of a mobile home trailer — had a large dent as if something big smashed into it. There were no windows on the front of the house, but it did have a porch with metal chain-link fence posts that served as porch roof supports. The house was a very bright yellow, and the roof was a hodgepodge of materials new and old.

They got out of the vehicle, and Eleanor gazed at the Pepper mansion in horror.

"Somebody lives here?" asked Eleanor.

"Yeah, Pepper."

"Is he the headless horseman or something?"

"No, he's a real person with a head and all."

"How did you ever meet him?"

"We went to high school together. I was the only one who would talk to him. Everyone else was scared of him. Come on."

Eleanor stood in place as Vegas started toward the house. She stopped when she realized her mother wasn't moving. "Are you coming?"

"I can wait out here. I might work on the vehicle a little. Give it a once-over and make sure the frog chain is still working and all."

"What in the world is a frog chain?" Vegas asked.

"It's what connects the steering wheel to the dashboard. Without it, the dashboard will fall off. I saw it on one of those shows where they buy an old car and rebuild it in about thirty minutes to sell at the end of the episode."

Vegas went back, grabbed her mother by the arm, and pulled her toward the house. "He won't bite."

"He won't clean either, apparently. Wait a minute, I've got to get Buttermilk."

Eleanor got Buttermilk, and the odd trio approached the house.

They stepped onto the porch and saw a box of plastic pumpkin heads that looked like part of a horror collection. And strung along the metal fence posts were string beans that looked like they'd been hanging there since last year.

"Do we really have to go inside?" asked Eleanor.

"It'll be fine. You'll see."

Vegas knocked on the door, and it was quickly opened by a large man. He had to be six-five and more than three hundred pounds, Eleanor thought. His frizzy hair was beet red, the same color as his full beard. He wore bib overalls, work boots that were untied, and a plaid shirt coat that seemed out of place on such a warm day.

Despite his Bigfoot appearance, Pepper was anything but a beast. He greeted Vegas with a big smile and said enthusiastically, "Vegas, I was wondering when you might come by again! Who did you bring with you?"

"This is Buttermilk and my mother," Vegas said.

"Nice to meet you. Interesting that you introduced the dog first," Pepper said.

Eleanor looked like she wanted to chime in, but she was visibly uncomfortable and simply said, "You have a very nice home, Mr. Pepper."

"No one has ever told me that before. I'm touched," Pepper replied. "So, Vegas, what do you want?"

"What makes you think I want something?"

"You never visit me unless you want something."

"She does the same thing to me," Eleanor said, feeling more comfortable now that she knew she had something in common with this giant.

"Well, I need to examine the court deeds to see who owns the Rhinehouse Apartments building. I went to the courthouse today, but they were closed because of a water leak."

"Come on in. But don't touch anything — it might blow up."

Pepper led the way inside as Eleanor grabbed Vegas by the arm and said earnestly, "We're going to die up here."

"Mom, we're not going to die. Besides, Buttermilk will protect you."

They both looked at the dog, who was asleep on the front porch. Vegas added, "Or not."

They walked into what was obviously a hoarder's house. Boxes were stacked to the ceiling, and there was stuff everywhere. A radio was blaring *Hush* by Deep Purple from somewhere in the small house.

Eleanor lost any semblance of comfort and shrieked as she saw first a spider, then a mouse, and then stuffed animal heads that appeared to have been Frankensteined together to form a strange beast.

She composed herself after a bit and whispered, "I don't understand how my beautiful daughter would ever allow herself to be associated with a person of such questionable character."

"He's fine, Mom, shh."

They walked over to Pepper, who was seated at his computer. He had ten monitors in front of him, all showing something different — security camera footage from an area outside the house, Fox Business Network, ESPN, *Aliens*, and more.

"Frisco Jones," Pepper said.

"Frisco Jones what?" Vegas asked.

"That's the person who owns the Rhinehouse Apartments."

"You already found it?"

"Yeah. He bought it a couple of years ago. Got it from the Homestand Corporation."

Vegas carefully stepped over several items on the floor and looked over Pepper's shoulder. "Does it give his address?"

"He lives on a boat. Blue Falls Marina, boat slit fifteen."

"A boat?" Eleanor said. "I've never met anyone that lives on a boat before. I know someone that lives in a camper, but not a boat."

Vegas ignored her and was about to ask another question when she noticed Pepper was scratched up.

"What happened to your face?"

"Oh, I tried to jump my house on a motorcycle," answered Pepper.

"Why would you do that?" Eleanor asked in horror.

"I saw an Evel Knievel biography on the History Channel and got inspired. I planned it out pretty well, ramp and everything, and I had a Honda two-fifty that ran great. I really thought I could make it."

"What happened?" Vegas said.

"I missed the ramp and ran the motorcycle into the front steps. It flipped me over the handlebars, and I ran smack dab into the door with my face."

"You could have been killed!" Eleanor said.

"No, I was wearing a helmet," replied Pepper.

"Why did you miss the ramp?" Vegas asked.

"Do you have eye problems?" added Eleanor.

"I do now."

"Sorry," Vegas said.

"So anyway, what's this Rhinehouse thing all about?" Pepper asked.

"A man named Wilson Hopkins died, and his brother thinks he was murdered. The police said it was an accident."

"Wilson Hopkins the chess player?"

"Yeah. You know him?" Vegas asked.

"Sure. I've competed against him," Pepper said. "Great chess player, but nobody really liked him. He was one of those guys that when he beat you, he would gloat and belittle you in front of everybody."

"That's not good sportsmanship," Eleanor said.

"I should interview some of his opponents," Vegas thought aloud. "If he's as bad as that, he definitely could have made some enemies."

"I'm going to a chess tournament Friday at Blue Falls High. You can come along if you'd like. It'll be like a date," Pepper said hopefully.

"Business meeting. I'll see you there," Vegas said. "Come on, Mom. And thanks again, Pepper."

12

The next afternoon, Vegas, Eleanor, and Buttermilk made a visit to the marina. People scurried about, getting their boats ready for an evening out on the water or putting things away after a day of boating.

"I wish I had a boat," Eleanor said.

"Daddy tried to get a boat one time, and you wouldn't let him," Vegas reminded her.

"That was a bass boat," Eleanor said. "That's different from these boats. These have a roof on them and a place to sleep. Your father just wanted to go out on the lake to get away from me. I wasn't going to allow that."

"Sounds like Dad and I are in the same boat."

"What?" Eleanor said.

"Never mind. If you had a boat, what would you name it?"

"That's an interesting question. I've never really

thought about it. Aren't they usually named after women or some sort of business interest like *Two for One*?"

"*Two for One*?"

"You have to name it something memorable," Eleanor said. "You have to admit that you would remember a boat named *Two for One*. And I think it describes our relationship perfectly."

Vegas shook her head and said, "If we ever get a boat together, you are not allowed to name it."

They walked along reading the numbers on the boat slits and became more and more confused as they went.

"These boat slit numbers aren't in order," Vegas said. "Why wouldn't they just number them from one to whatever it goes up to?"

"They were probably seasick when they were painting the numbers on the posts and just wanted to go back home and lie down," replied Eleanor. "I would never get on a boat in the open sea like this. It's just too dangerous. I'd worry constantly that the boat would sink or turn over. I just wouldn't feel comfortable at all."

"You just said a minute ago that you would like to have a boat," Vegas said.

"A boat, yes. On the sea, no."

"But look at it. It's beautiful out here," Vegas stated. "You could be hanging out with all the attractive rich people."

"The sea is beautiful from the land," Eleanor said, "but it's completely different on the water. Storms could come up without any notice. Seasickness is a big problem. As you can tell from the misnumbers on these boat slits."

"Misnumbers?"

"Well, I don't know what you call it when you number something wrong."

"Apparently."

They walked on, still looking for fifteen.

"There are monsters out there, too," blurted out Eleanor.

"You don't believe in sea monsters, do you?"

"Absolutely. I saw one."

"When would you have seen a sea monster?" Vegas asked. "You refuse to go out on the sea."

"I saw one on TV."

"TV doesn't count. You have to see it in person," Vegas said.

"It scared me so bad that I had to turn the channel."

Vegas stopped. "Hey, we're here. Boat slit fifteen."

"That didn't take as long as I thought it would," Eleanor said. "Time really does fly when you're having fun."

They both examined the boat. It was named *Frosty* and seemed to be on the verge of sinking. It sat low in the water, needed to be painted, and had several missing rungs on the ladder that went up to the top deck. It reminded both of them of a sunken ship.

"Is anyone on it?" asked Eleanor.

"If they are, they might want to get off of it," Vegas observed wryly.

"You'd think a man that owned an apartment building would have a better-looking boat," Eleanor said.

"The Rhinehouse Apartments building isn't much better than ole *Frosty* here."

"Who would name their boat *Frosty*? That's a name for snowmen and weather patterns."

"The boat looks kind of dangerous to me, don't you think?" Vegas asked. "Why wouldn't he take better care of his boat, being that it's the only thing that can get him back to the harbor?"

"Maybe he's hit on bad times. Owning a lot of properties can do that, you know. Hey, do you think that's why he lives on the boat? He's come into some money problems?"

Vegas was impressed. "That's a good theory. How did you come up with that?"

"From watching *Monk*," Eleanor said. "You know, I think he's a real detective."

"Whatever you say, Mom," Vegas replied as she looked around to see if there was any movement on board the boat.

Their eyes were drawn to some empty fuel cans in the near corner. There were seven of them, which Vegas found odd.

"I don't think anyone is here. Maybe we should go," Eleanor said.

"Not yet. There's a way to see if anyone is on a boat."

"Are you going to throw a rock or something?" Eleanor asked.

Vegas looked at her mother oddly and simply shouted, "Hello? Is anyone here?"

"Ahoy, mates," Eleanor added enthusiastically.

Vegas rolled her eyes and mumbled, "There she blows."

Just then, they heard movement inside the boat. A moment later, out walked an elderly man wearing a captain's hat; a buttoned-up, donkey-imprinted *Hee Haw* shirt; white shorts; and green flip-flops over white-sock-covered feet.

"Hello, ladies. Are you wanting to charter a boat for the day?" he asked with a big smile through his too-white teeth.

"No, thank you," Vegas said.

"That's a pretty dog you have there, ma'am," he said as he observed Buttermilk by Eleanor's side.

"Thank you," Eleanor said. "He's a basset hound. I think that's Latin for sleep."

The man laughed and said, "I once had a dog, but I lost him."

"I'm sorry to hear that. How did you lose him?"

"Let's just say Frisbees and boats don't go together."

Vegas interrupted their conversation and asked, "Are you Frisco Jones?"

He looked at her surprised. "Depends on what you want."

"Do you own the Rhinehouse Apartments building?"

"Yes, but if you're having problems with your neighbors, you can talk to the security guard. The guy who was running my properties is in jail right now for fixing catfights, so it'll have to be the security guard. Or maybe one of the janitors. Janitors think they know everything anyway."

"I'm not here about noisy neighbors. I'm Vegas Chantly, and I'm a private investigator."

"Private investigator? Who hired a private investigator?" asked Frisco.

"Bosco Hopkins," Vegas said.

"Never heard of him."

"He's one of your tenants," Vegas informed him.

"I don't know the people that live in my apartments. I have about fifty properties, including apartment buildings, motels, restaurants, and this charter service, which I have to admit is my favorite, at least when she's working. I once owned a funeral home for a day, but it creeped me out too much, and I sold it right back to the person I bought it from. But I have people that run all that for me now. I'm trying to enjoy my life."

"Someone bought back a funeral home in a day?" Vegas asked.

"Well, it held fond memories for him. He had buried a lot of his family there."

"Uh, yes, I see," Vegas said. "Well, I was hired by Bosco Hopkins to look into the death of his brother. Did anyone tell you about that?"

"People die all the time. Nobody needs to tell me that."

"It was in your apartment building," Eleanor said. "Wouldn't you want to know that?"

"Not really. Kind of creeps me out, actually. I don't like death. Or noodles. I find both of them eerie as all get out. But what does this have to do with me?"

"I talked to your security guard and asked to see the security camera, and he told me he couldn't show it to me unless I got permission from you."

"Permission granted," he said with a jolly laugh. "Now, can I get you two something? A couple martinis? And maybe something for your dog — are you sure he's not dead?" Frisco said as he looked down at Buttermilk.

"I'm sure," Eleanor said, but then nudged him with her shoe. "No, he's not."

"I was wondering if you could call the security guard and give him permission to show me the security footage," Vegas said.

"I told you that you could see it."

"He won't believe me. He seemed a little cocky."

Frisco nodded and said, "Sounds like a janitor. All right, I can do that," he said as he pulled his cellphone out of his pocket and sat on the edge of his boat.

"His name is Jim Bob Cooter," Vegas said.

This brought a confused look from Frisco Jones. "Jim Bob Cooter? That's not the name of my security guard."

"What? I was just there. That's what he said his name was."

"William Jennings is my security guard. I have no idea who Jim Bob Cooter is. Sounds like a character from that old show *Dukes of Hazzard.*"

"Wait, who's a duke?" asked Eleanor.

"Mom, not now," Vegas pleaded. "Have you ever had problems with Jennings?"

"Oh, yeah. He thinks he owns the apartment building. He's always buying things and charging them to the company without my permission. He does my books, too, so he thinks he can get away with it, I guess."

"If you don't trust him, then why don't you fire him?" Vegas asked.

"You can't just fire your son-in-law. Too many things can go wrong with the home life."

Jones called the number to the apartments.

"William, this is Frisco. Two very attractive women and a dead dog are here asking to look at some security footage. I want you to let them see it."

Jones listened to his security guard respond. A surprised look flashed across his face and he said, "That's interesting."

"What's interesting?" Eleanor asked Vegas.

"I'm not on the other end of the line, Mom."

Jones put his hand over the microphone and said, "The police are there now looking at the footage."

Vegas and Eleanor looked at each other, said goodbye to Jones, and quickly headed out. Or at least as quickly as Buttermilk would allow.

13

Vegas and Eleanor pulled into the Rhinehouse Apartments parking lot about twenty minutes later. A black-and-white patrol car was positioned near the entrance, so they knew the police were still there. Eleanor parked her SUV between the patrol car and an unmarked police car. She got out and opened the rear door to retrieve Buttermilk.

"Mom, can't you leave that dog in the vehicle?" Vegas said.

"He's part of our team. Besides, you're not supposed to leave your children in the car unattended."

"You're not even a part of the team," Vegas said.

"I drove us here, so that makes me and everything inside my vehicle officially part of the team." She turned to Buttermilk and cooed, "Isn't that right, baby?"

Vegas sighed and just then saw Sergeant Miller exit the apartment building.

"Sergeant Miller!" Vegas called out as she walked toward him.

"Yes?" he said. He looked as if he was trying to remember who she was.

"I'm Vegas Chantly. I spoke to you earlier about—"

"Honey!" Eleanor yelled from her vehicle.

Vegas turned around and saw that her mother had gotten Buttermilk's leash caught around the steering wheel and her neck and couldn't get loose.

"I'm hung up!" Eleanor yelled, and then Vegas heard her say, "Bad dog."

"Excuse me a moment," Vegas said to Sergeant Miller and ran to her help her mother.

"How did this happen?" Vegas asked.

"I was making sure I got my keys out of the ignition when Buttermilk jumped the seat, and the next thing I knew, I was all wrapped up around the steering wheel."

"Bringing you along is like not being able to find something that you really need," Vegas said as she freed the leash from the steering wheel.

"Oh, thank goodness. I almost choked to death," Eleanor said and rubbed her throat. "I didn't know he could jump like that with those little legs. Maybe he used to be Spider-Man's dog."

"Please don't cause any more trouble, or I'm going to have to take both of you back to the pet store," Vegas said and turned and ran into Sergeant Miller. Vegas shrieked in surprise, which startled her mother, who screamed, which scared Buttermilk, who began to bark.

"Sorry, I didn't mean to scare you," Sergeant Miller said. "I had to come over and take a look."

"Everything is fine now," Vegas said. "Oh, who am I kidding, nothing is ever fine when you add a dog and a mother to your day. ... Did you see the security camera footage?"

Sergeant Miller looked puzzled but then put everything together. "Ah, this was the wiener place you spoke about down at the office."

"Yeah, but forget the wieners. This is my client's apartment building. What did you find on the security footage?" Vegas asked. "Did anyone go into apartment fifteen?

"There was no security footage," Sergeant Miller said.

"But there are security cameras on both corners of the building," Vegas said in surprise. "A security guard also mentioned that the hallway has cameras."

"When we reviewed the footage, it was all snow. The guard said they malfunctioned somehow. But we only had access to the outside cameras. He said the cameras in the hallway had been removed."

"Removed? When?" Vegas asked.

"Said they never worked right, so they took them down."

"What about the outside cameras? Are they working?" Vegas asked.

"Yes, they seem to be working now, but there's no recorded footage."

"Don't you find it odd that they don't have a recording of anything?"

"I'm finding a lot of odd things today," Sergeant Miller said as he walked away.

"Wait a minute," Vegas said.

Sergeant Miller stopped and said in an annoyed tone, "What now, lady?"

"Why are you here? You don't even believe anything happened here. You think that Wilson Hopkins died in an accident."

"We got a call that a body had been found in the basement," Sergeant Miller said.

"Body?" a stunned Vegas replied. "What body? Do you know who it is?"

"His name is Billy Sanchez. He's the janitor."

Shock showed on the faces of Vegas and Eleanor.

"He was the one we spoke to the first day we came here," Eleanor said. "He wore these tight jeans that made him look—"

"Uh, we know what he looks like, ma'am," Sergeant Miller said.

"Sorry," Eleanor said. "At my age, you always remember men in tight jeans."

"Who found him?" Vegas asked.

"The security guard found him when he was doing his rounds."

"What did he die from?"

"Smoke inhalation. There was a fire in the basement. It appears that Sanchez was asleep when the fire started, and the smoke killed him."

"Was he lying on the floor?" Vegas asked.

"No, on the couch. He must have been taking a nap."

"I would like to take a look around and—"

Sergeant Miller abruptly interrupted Vegas. "That's a cordoned-off area. No one is allowed down there."

"But this is my case," pleaded Vegas.

"I don't mean any offense, ladies, but you need to leave the investigating to professionals," he said.

At that moment, the security guard came running out of the front of the building shouting for the sergeant. He was waving something in his hand.

"What is it?" Sergeant Miller asked.

"You dropped your badge in the basement," he said and handed it to the sergeant.

Eleanor looked at Vegas as if to ask if this was the security guard she had previously talked to. She shook her head and asked the man, "You're the security guard?"

"Yeah. I'm William Jennings."

"What happened to Jim Bob Cooter? He was working security when I came here before."

"I don't know who you're talking about, we don't have a Cooter here. I've been the security guard for several years now. My father-in-law owns the apartment building, and he doesn't have any other security guards."

"No, you're lying," Vegas said.

The security guard looked upset. "What do you mean I'm lying? I'm the security guard. There's no one else."

"When I came here the other day, you weren't here. Where were you?" Vegas asked.

"What day?" he asked.

"Day before yesterday."

"Uh ... I ..." The guard stumbled for answers but didn't find any.

"Tell us the truth, son," Sergeant Miller said.

He sighed. "Okay, sometimes I bring in another guy to watch the place during the day."

"Why would you do that?" Vegas asked.

"I get bored. There's nothing to do. You simply do the same thing day after day. So I told him I'd pay him fifty dollars if he would come in and just watch the security cameras and answer the phones and such."

"What's his name?" the sergeant asked.

"Jim Bob Cooter," Jennings said in a depressed voice.

"Oh, you know him, honey!" Eleanor said to Vegas, who rolled her eyes.

"What do you do when he's doing your job?" Sergeant Miller asked.

"I skateboard and surf."

"Skateboard and surf?" Vegas asked incredulously. "What are you, ten years old?"

"That's my passion. I love doing it and don't want to spend my entire life doing something that I hate. It's not right for a man to spend his life that way. I want to be happy, and skateboarding and surfing make me happy. I wasn't hurting anybody."

"Frisco Jones was paying you to do a job you weren't doing," Vegas said.

"Well, when you put it that way. ... But the job was getting done, just not by me. Then this happened."

"Was he the one on duty when Wilson Hopkins' body was found?" Sergeant Miller asked.

"Yeah. He hid when the police got here because he was afraid we'd get into trouble. He didn't even know anything was wrong until he saw the police walk in. I guess Bosco called them."

"What about the security footage?" Vegas asked. "What happened to that?"

"I'm not sure. He didn't tell me much, just that he hid under the desk when the cops came. Maybe he hit something by mistake on the computer or kicked a cord out or something. He's not very smart. He thinks he is, but he's really not," Jennings said.

"Do you know where he is now?" Vegas said.

"Or where he lives?" Eleanor asked.

"I don't know where he went or lives. Said he just wanted to get away from the world for a while. Being a security guard can take a lot out of you. You know, patrolling, finding bodies, bringing the police their badges and stuff."

Vegas asked, "How did you and Jim Bob meet?"

"At the beach. We were hanging out down there, and I told him about how boring my job was, and he said he didn't have a job, and that's how our little plan came together."

A detective approached Sergeant Miller. "Sergeant, can I speak with you for a minute?"

"Yeah."

The two of them stepped away and Vegas turned to the security guard and asked, "What did the police look at?"

"Just the basement," Jennings said.

"And there's no security camera footage at all?" Vegas asked.

"No. Everything is looped over every twenty-four hours anyway. So even if the cameras were working properly, there wouldn't have been any footage from the night of Wilson Hopkins' death. The camera company is supposed to come out tomorrow and either fix them or replace them."

"They certainly better. Who knows what might happen if they're broken," Eleanor said.

Sergeant Miller walked back to the group and asked the security guard, "Did Sanchez play chess?"

"I don't think so. He once told me that the man upstairs kept challenging him to a game, but he hated chess. And he found the guy rather annoying."

"That would be Wilson Hopkins," Vegas said. "Sanchez told us the same thing when we got here the first day."

"He asked me to play, too, and called me a coward when I told him I wasn't interested," Jennings said.

"Well, the police found a chess trophy in Sanchez's apartment," the sergeant informed them.

"Interesting," Vegas said. "A trophy was missing from Wilson's apartment."

"It had blood on the base of it. Looks like you might have been right all along — Wilson Hopkins was murdered, and Billy Sanchez did it," the sergeant said.

14

"I don't think he did it," Vegas said as she sat on the bed in her camper, taking a bite of a thickly glazed doughnut.

"He didn't seem like a killer to me," Eleanor said as she sat in the patio chair and put Buttermilk in her lap.

"If he hated chess, then why would he steal a chess trophy?" Vegas asked. "Why would anybody steal a chess trophy, for that matter? If you didn't win it, what good is it to you?"

Eleanor slowly stroked Buttermilk's head. He was already dozing.

"Maybe he knew it had blood on it, so he was trying to hide it," Eleanor volunteered.

"If you kill somebody with a trophy, why in the world would you take it back to your own apartment? You would dispose of it somewhere else," Vegas said. "I need the police to tell me whether or not the blood on the trophy belongs to Wilson Hopkins."

"Who else could it belong to?"

Vegas reached over to the table and tore off a paper towel to clean her hands of her doughnut residue. "I don't know, but man, I wish that Sergeant Miller would have let me go down in the basement to look around," Vegas said, taking a sip of coffee.

"What would you have been looking for?"

"How the fire started. That's a key to seeing if it was an accident or not," Vegas said. "You just don't know what you'll find when you look at a scene like that."

"I don't think I would go into a basement with a dead body," Eleanor said. "That's just too weird for me."

Vegas repositioned herself in her bed and placed her back against the back wall of the camper.

"Why would a couch be in a basement?" Vegas asked. "Was it set up for an apartment down there? Was it where they threw all the junk the tenants left behind? Going down there would have given me some perspective on whether or not it was an accident."

"But the police will figure it out," Eleanor said. "You seem like you don't trust them."

"They have tons of cases. I just have this one, and I can concentrate on it fully. Kind of." She shot her mother a look and continued. "Remember, they thought Wilson's death was an accident. Now, with the trophy found in Sanchez's apartment, and with what Miller said, it looks like they'll say he killed Wilson and that will be the end of it."

"Why couldn't it be Sanchez?" Eleanor asked.

"It just isn't adding up. Too many things are happening here, like someone is trying to tidy things up after the fact."

"Do you think Jim Bob Cooter killed Sanchez?"

"He's my leading suspect right now. Why did he disappear? He just left without telling anybody. ... I just don't think Sanchez killed Wilson because he found him annoying."

"But why would Jim Bob Cooter be involved in this? Does he like chess so much that he stole the trophy, and Sanchez found out, so Jim Bob Cooter killed him? I really like saying the name Jim Bob Cooter, don't you?"

"Not really," Vegas said as she crossed her arms on her stomach and sucked her teeth, then picked them with her fingernail to get out a piece of doughnut.

Eleanor stroked Buttermilk's head and asked, "Can I have a doughnut?"

"Yeah," Vegas said as she got up to grab a doughnut from the box on the counter. She pulled one out of its row and handed it to Eleanor. Buttermilk immediately woke up and looked at the treat.

"You can't have Mommy's doughnut now," Eleanor said as she tried to eat it while fending off a persistent Buttermilk.

"If the police confirm the blood on the trophy is Wilson's, that still doesn't necessarily mean that Sanchez did it," Vegas said, thinking hard and staring off into space. "Someone else could have done it, then placed the trophy in the apartment and killed Sanchez. Perhaps it's even Sanchez's blood."

"I thought the fire killed him," Eleanor said as she surrendered the rest of her doughnut to Buttermilk, who gulped it down in a matter of seconds.

"Just because someone is found dead in a fire doesn't mean it was the fire that killed him."

"How else could he have died?"

"Like Buttermilk's desire for doughnuts, the possibilities are endless," Vegas said as she watched the dog lick glazing off his face.

"Well, if Billy Sanchez didn't do it, then who do you think did?"

"Jim Bob Cooter seems the most likely suspect for this murder, too. Why wouldn't he show us the footage or even tell us the name of the owner of the apartment complex? He could have answered all of my questions, and I would never have known he wasn't the real security guard."

"Maybe it's like the real security guard said, what's his name," Eleanor said.

"William Jennings."

"Yeah, him. Jim Bob Cooter could have accidentally messed up the cameras when he hid under the desk, or maybe he just forgot to turn them on."

"Forgot to turn them on?" Vegas said as if she didn't think that made any sense whatsoever.

"The other day I put a chicken pot pie in the microwave and came back ten minutes later and noticed that I forgot to turn it on. It can happen. And remember, he wasn't the real security guard, so he probably didn't know what he was doing."

"But a security camera is on all the time. Surely it wouldn't be so simple to just turn it off or erase it without anyone knowing about it."

"Maybe he didn't erase it. Maybe he stole the tape out of it and threw it in the trash out back."

"Everything is digital now. I don't even know if they sell videotapes anymore."

"They quit making videotapes?" Eleanor asked.

"Yeah," Vegas said.

"That's sad," Eleanor replied. "Another part of my culture is gone."

Vegas then remembered something. "Hey, Jennings said that it's on a twenty-four-hour loop, that it records over itself every twenty-four hours."

"I remember him saying that, yes," Eleanor said.

"Maybe it is a video then. The apartment building doesn't look like it's kept in the best of shape — that's probably a sign that the security cameras are old. Maybe it was as simple as pulling out a video with incriminating evidence on it and slipping another video in its place."

Eleanor said, "Didn't Jennings say the video was all squiggly?"

"Yeah, he did. So he either erased it and put it back in the recorder, or he put in a bad tape and disposed of the incriminating one."

They were both quiet for a moment as they thought things over. Then Eleanor said, "You know who I think it was?"

"Who?"

"Bosco."

"I don't think Bosco would kill his own brother."

"He was jealous of his success. He probably thought Mom liked Wilson best. Got all the good school clothes when they were kids, and he was just left with hand-me-downs."

"What are you talking about?" Vegas said.

"It's just a theory. Me and Buttermilk will probably figure it out. We're becoming a really good team, you know."

"You two seem to need each other. All right, I think I'll get to bed."

"Bed? What time is it?" Eleanor asked.

Vegas glanced at her Popeye alarm clock. "Ten-thirty."

"Wow, it's later than I thought," she said and started to stand up. Buttermilk reluctantly got off her lap and stepped down to the floor. "What are your plans for tomorrow?"

"I'm going to go visit our new friend Sergeant Miller and see what he learned at Sanchez's apartment," Vegas said as she turned down the covers on her bed.

"What time do you want me to come and pick you up tomorrow?"

"You don't have to pick me up, I've got a car now."

"I'll come anyway. I haven't ridden in the car yet. Then tomorrow evening we can go out to dinner. We haven't done that in a while."

"I can't tomorrow night," Vegas said as she opened a drawer by her sink and pulled out her toothbrush and a tube of Colgate.

"Why not?"

"I got a date."

"A date!" Eleanor said in an excited voice. "With who?"

"About one hundred nerds."

15

Vegas, Eleanor, and Buttermilk pulled into the police station parking lot in the Trans Am. As Vegas turned off the car, Buttermilk began barking.

"Shh," Eleanor said. "He thinks we're going to the Sugar Shack for doggie ice cream."

"Why did you have to bring the dog?" Vegas asked as she shook her head.

"He's helping us solve the case. See, you're Batman, Buttermilk is Robin, and I'm Daphne."

"Daphne?" Vegas asked confusedly. "Who's Daphne?"

"The cute redhead on *Scooby-Doo*," Eleanor informed her. "You don't remember *Scooby-Doo*?"

Vegas shook her head in frustration. "How is this dog helping me solve my case? All he does is eat and sleep."

"Dogs solve crimes all the time. You really should watch more cartoons" Eleanor said.

Vegas looked in the backseat at Buttermilk, who was still barking.

"I don't think he could find his own dog dish," Vegas said.

"He doesn't have to find it, Mommy will bring it to him. Won't I, Buttermilk?"

"Can you make him stop barking?"

"Stop barking!" Eleanor shouted. "Stop barking! Stop barking, Buttermilk. Stop! Stop barking! It's annoying! I'll show you!"

Eleanor barked at Buttermilk.

"That, uh, wasn't what I had in mind," Vegas said, wondering what strangers would say if they saw a woman barking at a dog.

Suddenly, Buttermilk stopped barking.

"Thank God," Vegas said, her hands pressed together prayerfully.

"I think he's about to pee," Eleanor observed.

"Get him out of the car!" Vegas screamed as they quickly picked up Buttermilk and sat him beside the car so he could do his business.

"That must be what the barking was for," Eleanor said. "See, we're learning about each other. Every time he barks, we'll know to get him out of your car."

"Wonderful. I'm going in now. You can stay out here with Scooby or Robin or whatever you want to call him."

"We'll come with you," Eleanor said and grabbed Buttermilk's leash.

"They don't allow dogs in police stations."

"But he's a working dog."

Vegas looked down at Buttermilk, who was already settling in for a nap.

"Well, sometimes he's a working dog," Eleanor said.

"He's never a working dog. He's just a tired dog," Vegas said.

"The police have German shepherds, so I'm sure they wouldn't care if I brought Buttermilk inside," Eleanor said. "If the police brought their German shepherds into my house, I wouldn't mind."

"If the police bring a German shepherd into your house, I think you might soon have some legal problems," Vegas pointed out.

Eleanor pulled on Buttermilk's leash. "Come on, boy. Get up for Mommy. We're going to go play with the police now."

Buttermilk got up as Vegas looked at her mother and asked, "Play with the police?"

"I don't want to scare him. Going inside a police station can be stressful."

Eleanor looked down at Buttermilk, who was now between her legs, and asked Vegas, "Is he lying down or standing up? I can't always tell when I'm looking at him from this angle. You know, with his tiny legs and all."

"Let's go, crazy woman," Vegas said as the three of them went into the police station. They made their way to Sergeant Miller's office, and Vegas knocked on the door.

"Come in!" shouted an annoyed voice from the other side.

"He doesn't sound like he's in a good mood," Vegas said.

"He will be once he knows it's us," Eleanor said as Vegas opened the door.

The sergeant looked up from his paperwork and said gruffly, "Why are you two here?"

"My Wilson Hopkins case, remember? Did you hear back about the blood on the trophy yet?" asked Vegas.

"Not yet."

"How did Sanchez die?"

"I'm sure it was from the fire," the sergeant said.

Vegas continued her interrogation. "Were there any markings on him from a struggle? Was he hit with anything?"

"Not that I recall."

"Don't you think that's odd?" Vegas asked.

"He could have died from a heart attack or something."

"Heart attack?" Eleanor exclaimed. "He was a young man."

"It happens," Sergeant Miller replied. "Perhaps the fire stressed him out so much that it happened that way. The report should come in today, though."

"I thought you said he was taking a nap on the couch when the fire got started," Vegas said.

"It's possible," the sergeant said with a shrug. "We'll know soon. Now, if you would excuse me—"

"I don't think Sanchez did it," Vegas interrupted.

The sergeant sighed. "The trophy was missing from Wilson's apartment and was found in Sanchez's apartment," he reminded her. "It has blood on it."

"If he killed Wilson with the trophy, then why would he take it with him and stash it in his house?" Vegas asked.

"It was probably a trophy for him," said Eleanor, which brought a puzzled look from both Vegas and the sergeant. She realized what she said and replied, "Oh, my goodness, I made a funny! I mean killers sometimes take things from murder scenes and call them trophies." She laughed but stopped when she saw Vegas and the sergeant didn't find it amusing. "Carry on."

"He probably took the trophy to hide it — it was the murder weapon," the sergeant said.

"But he left his hat in the closet," Vegas pointed out. "Why wouldn't he have gone back for that?"

Sergeant Miller said, "Listen, when a man commits a murder, they say there are twenty things he needs to do afterward, but a person can only remember six of them. People watch all of these forensic shows on TV and think they know how to commit the perfect murder, but they don't take into account the emotional explosion that'll take place after they commit the act."

"I love those forensic shows," Eleanor said. "Me and Buttermilk watched one last night about a man that was obsessed with women's feet and—"

"Mom," Vegas pleaded, "we don't want to know what you and Buttermilk do at night. Okay?"

"I was just trying to help," she said. "He also thought the big toe on his right foot looked like his mother, so he would never wear socks or shoes on that foot because he worried he would smother her."

Vegas stared at her mother and asked, "Are you done?"

Eleanor nodded.

"I can't believe you don't think the janitor did it," Sergeant Miller said.

"I don't think he did it either," Eleanor said.

"And why not?"

"I think he's too handsome."

"That's your reason?" a stunned Sergeant Miller asked.

Eleanor thought it over then said confidently, "Yes. Yes, it is."

"Did you two escape from some sort of mental institution?" the sergeant mumbled.

Vegas sat down in the chair across from the sergeant's desk and said, "He has no motive to kill Wilson."

"Sometimes people are killed simply for being annoying," the sergeant said.

Eleanor laughed nervously.

"Well," Vegas began, "I think we have to talk with Jim Bob Cooter."

"Who?" the sergeant asked.

"The other security guard. He's the one that wouldn't let me look at the security footage and told me I had to get permission from the owner of the apartment building."

"That doesn't mean he's the killer. In fact, that doesn't sound like a bad reason at all. You're not law enforcement. You can't just demand to see security footage and expect to see it. Even from a fill-in security guard."

"Maybe he hadn't deleted the evidence yet and didn't want me to see it," Vegas said.

"You think he erased the footage after you left?" asked the sergeant.

"It's very possible," Vegas said.

The phone rang and the sergeant answered. "Sergeant Miller. ... Interesting. ... Are you sure? ... Okay, thanks."

The sergeant hung up and Vegas quickly asked, "Was that about the case?"

"What makes you think it was for you?" Sergeant Miller asked.

"It's always for her," Eleanor said.

"Well, that was the security camera people. They went out this morning and looked at their equipment at the Rhinehouse Apartments. They figured out what happened."

Eleanor and Vegas anxiously stared at the sergeant, waiting for him to say what it was. After a moment, they asked in unison, "What?"

"It was erased."

"It had to be Jim Bob Cooter!" Vegas said.

"It doesn't have to be Jim Bob Cooter. But that's where I'm going to start," Sergeant Miller said and got up from his desk. Vegas and Eleanor followed him to the door.

"Do you have his address?" Vegas asked.

"Yes. Now, where do you two think you're going?" Sergeant Miller asked.

"There are three of us actually," Eleanor said as she looked at her dog. "You forgot about Robin."

"Who?" the sergeant asked.

"Just ignore her. We're coming with you," Vegas said.

"No, I'm going alone. You two and Robin here go do whatever it is you do. Good day," the sergeant said and left.

"What do we do now?" Eleanor asked. "Go through his drawers?"

"Go through his drawers?!"

"He might have some evidence we could use on our case."

"No, we're going to leave the sergeant's drawers alone," Vegas said.

"What are we going to do then?"

"C'mon, Daphne and Robin — we're going to follow him."

16

Sergeant Miller pulled into a narrow, concrete driveway in a subdivision outside of Blue Falls. He got out of his car and scanned the lot. It was well taken care of, lawn mowed, shrubs neatly trimmed. He proceeded to head toward the front door when he heard a dog barking. He stopped in his tracks. "Oh, no."

He looked toward the corner of the lot and saw the tops of the heads of Vegas and Eleanor sticking above some shrubs. He saw Eleanor's head bob up and down several times. Evidently, she was trying to quiet her barking dog.

The sergeant shook his head and walked over to them, despair etched on his face.

"What are you two doing?"

Neither woman had seen or heard him arrive, and they both jumped in surprise.

"Shoot, I think he saw us," Eleanor said in frustration.

"Of course he saw us," Vegas retorted. "If you would

have squatted down like I told you to, then he wouldn't have noticed us."

"I'm at that age now that I can't squat very well. Something could bust or go flying across the yard."

"I didn't see you at first, your dog gave you away," the sergeant said.

"Why do you have to bring that stupid dog everywhere with us?" Vegas asked.

"He's helping us," Eleanor said.

"Helping get us caught," Vegas said as she looked at Buttermilk and said, "Bad dog."

"Why are you two here?" the sergeant asked frustratedly.

"I think it's obvious. We're following you," Vegas said.

"Why?"

"Because this has to do with my case. Our client's brother was murdered, at least I'm pretty sure he was murdered, and the person I think did it lives in that house. It's my job to put all the pieces together and make sure justice is served," Vegas said.

"That was beautiful," Eleanor said.

Sergeant Miller didn't think so, however. "You're interfering with an officer of the law. That's a crime. Not to mention that it's also dangerous for you and me."

Eleanor shook her head and caught Vegas' eye. "He sounds just like you when you're talking to me."

"That's different," Vegas said.

"The only difference is that he says it with a deep voice," Eleanor said. "He sounds like he's speaking through a water pipe or something. Can you say, 'Luke, I am your daddy?'"

"No. Now you two get out from behind that bush before someone calls the police," ordered the sergeant. "Then I want you to go home or back to the institution, whichever one is closer."

Vegas, Eleanor, and Buttermilk came out, and they dusted themselves off.

"I don't have time to fool with crazy right now," the sergeant said and headed toward Jim Bob Cooter's house.

"I'll come with you," Vegas said.

"You'll stay right there," the sergeant said in a forceful voice, which caused Vegas to put her hands up in surrender to indicate she understood.

Eleanor whispered to Vegas, "What kind of name is Jim Bob Cooter anyway?"

"Irish?" Vegas guessed.

Meanwhile, Sergeant Miller knocked on the door and waited for a reply. He received no answer and knocked louder as Vegas walked to the side of the house, with her mother and Buttermilk uncomfortably close behind. Vegas stopped at the first window she came to and peered inside. The house was on a sloping lot, so Vegas had to stand on her toes to see through the window.

"What's in there?" Eleanor asked.

"Keep your voice down," Vegas said in a whisper. "We don't want a murder suspect to catch us peeping in his house."

Eleanor whispered back. "What did you say?"

"Be quiet," Vegas scolded and tried to get more height by standing on her tippy toes.

"What do you see?"

"It looks like the living room."

"I want to see," Eleanor said and stepped to the window. She stood on her tippy toes, too, but couldn't see in very well. "Can you boost me up?"

"How do I do that?"

"Just get on your hands and knees and let me stand on you like a stool."

"No thanks," Vegas replied. "Hold on a second, I think I saw a bucket over there." She retrieved the bucket, a sturdy orange five-gallon one, and helped her mother stand on it to see into the house.

"It looks like your camper — nothing but a mess," Eleanor said.

"My camper isn't that messy."

"Your whole camper is smaller than his living room. You should have been a fake security guard instead of a private investigator."

"Why's that?"

"Because fake security guards can afford this house."

Vegas ignored her mother's comments. "There's a car in the driveway."

"Do you think it's his?"

"I assume it is. I'm going to look in another window."

Vegas walked to a window near a heat pump. There was a cinder block near the pump, so she dragged it to the window and stood on it. She slowly began to raise her head to peek inside when her mother whispered, "Vegas. Vegas. I got Buttermilk's leash hung up on the heat pump."

Vegas stepped off the block and helped her mother get Buttermilk loose.

"You need to keep this dog at the house or start carrying him around in a backpack," Vegas whispered.

"I never thought of a backpack. That might work. Or maybe a stroller," Eleanor whispered back.

"What are you two still doing here?" a loud voice asked from behind, sending their hearts racing. They both looked around and saw a furious-looking Sergeant Miller.

"You've got to stop doing that," Eleanor said.

"Let's calm down now," Vegas said.

"Yeah, yelling like that isn't good for your heart — or mine," Eleanor added. "You even scared Buttermilk so bad I don't think he can ever sleep again." She then noticed that her dog, in fact, was sound asleep. "Nope, I was wrong."

"You two aren't supposed to be here. This is a police investigation, not a housewarming party," the sergeant said sternly.

"This is my investigation, too," Vegas said. "An investigation that you didn't believe in to start with, so I'm going to investigate it, and I don't care how loud you get either."

Vegas and the sergeant stared hard at each other in a silent standoff. Eleanor tried to calm things down by suggesting, "Maybe we should concentrate on the case itself instead of the participants investigating it. Now, Sergeant Miller, did anyone come to the door when you were knocking on it?"

"No. Nobody answered."

Eleanor turned to her daughter and asked, "Vegas, did you see anyone in the window when you looked inside?"

"No. But I didn't get to look in the other window."

"And why was that?" asked Eleanor.

"Because some crazy woman got her dog hung up on the heat pump."

Eleanor frowned and said, "I'm sure she was doing the best she could."

Vegas rolled her eyes and walked back to the second window, with the sergeant and Eleanor following her. Vegas stepped on the cinderblock, put her hands on the window ledge to steady herself, then pressed her face against the window and used her hands to see inside better.

"What do you see?" the sergeant asked.

"A bedroom."

"Is it clean?" Eleanor asked.

Vegas and the sergeant looked at each other. Vegas shrugged and responded, "Why on Earth would you ask that?"

"It's something all mothers want to know," Eleanor said.

Vegas kept looking inside, and she was soon joined at the window by the sergeant, who was tall enough to simply look in. Eleanor started jumping up and down beside them. The sergeant looked at her.

"What are you doing?" he asked.

"I'm trying to see inside. Maybe I could get on your back?"

He sighed and said, "Fine, get on."

Vegas, who had been looking intently inside, turned to

speak and saw her mother sitting piggyback on Sergeant Miller. Her jaw dropped.

"What do you see?" the sergeant asked, as if giving mothers a piggyback ride was completely normal.

"Look at the foot of the bed. Do you see that?" Vegas asked as she stared back through the bedroom window.

"What is it?" the sergeant asked.

"Is that somebody's foot?" Vegas wondered aloud.

"A foot by the foot of the bed," Eleanor said. "That seems important."

"Maybe," the sergeant said through gritted teeth. "Okay, I can't hold you up anymore, you have to get down."

"Sorry," Eleanor said and released her grip on his shoulders.

The sergeant then slowly raised the window, and when it was open several inches, an overwhelming stench and a wave of heat hit them in their faces.

Vegas made a gagging sound and said, "Is the furnace on?"

"It sure sounds like it," the sergeant said.

"Why would the furnace be on? It's almost ninety degrees today," Eleanor observed.

Vegas told the sergeant, "Give me a boost."

"You can't go in there," he said.

"I'm the only one who can fit through the window," Vegas said.

"I'm offended by that comment, Vegas," Eleanor said. "I've been doing aerobics lately."

"You have?" Vegas asked.

"Well, standing aerobics. All you need is a wall or a big

stick to push against. It's kind of like standing-still aerobics."

Vegas turned back to the window and said again, "I can fit in there."

"I can't let you go inside — there could be someone else in there," the sergeant said.

"Someone has to go inside," Vegas said.

"I'll go," he said and grabbed the bottom of the window frame and tried to pull himself up. The ensuing struggle was embarrassing for all three of them. His massive six-five frame wasn't working the way he had intended. He attempted to take his right leg and lift it onto the window frame and try to pull himself in, but every time he lifted his size-fifteen shoe, it banged into the side of the house with a noise that sounded like a blacksmith hitting his hammer against iron.

"You look like you're trying to kickstart the house," Vegas observed.

"Be quiet," the sergeant said. "I'm concentrating."

Eleanor turned to Vegas and said, "Should we push him on in?"

"Maybe we should call the fire department," Vegas said as again and again, he failed to get his right leg up.

Sergeant Miller let go of the frame and fell backward onto the ground. Eleanor looked at him with motherly concern. "Are you okay?"

"Just humiliated is all," the sergeant replied as he got back to his feet.

"I'm going in," Vegas said.

"No," said the sergeant. "Someone else might be in there."

"It's probably safe. Your banging on the house with your foot probably scared them off," Eleanor said.

"I don't think anyone is in there with the furnace running full blast," Vegas said and pulled herself through the window. Carefully she walked to the bed to look at the foot. She gasped when she saw a man laying face up on the floor with a piece of paper on his chest. She wasn't sure if he was dead or simply unconscious. But one thing she did know was that it was Jim Bob Cooter.

"Hello?" Vegas asked, not sure if his waking up would be a good thing or not. What if he woke up and attacked her for intruding?

He didn't move. She knelt down and felt his hands. They were warm, though she assumed it was from the furnace running on high.

Vegas picked up the paper that was on his chest, read it, and walked back to the window to where her mother and the sergeant stood waiting.

"It's Jim Bob Cooter. He's dead."

"What's that paper?" the sergeant asked.

"It's a confession. It says, 'I killed Wilson Hopkins and Billy Sanchez. Please forgive me. Jim Bob Cooter.' But it's not signed, just typed out."

They were all quiet for a moment, pondering what this new evidence meant, until Eleanor broke the silence.

"Well, that's a kick in the pants," she said.

17

A t seven o'clock in the evening, Vegas parked her Trans Am in front of Blue Falls High School. She grabbed her hand purse from the passenger's seat and headed toward the gym.

She was wearing blue jeans, a cotton short-sleeve shirt, and soft-soled shoes. For the first time in what seemed like ages, her mother and Buttermilk stayed home. She had the evening all to herself — though with about one hundred chess nerds.

"Vegas!" a voice shouted from behind her. She turned and saw Pepper jogging at her. He was wearing a dark suit jacket, plaid pants, a white shirt, no tie, and work boots. The suit was about three times too small for his hulking frame.

"You came," Pepper said excitedly. "I figured you'd come to your senses and back out."

"I had to come for the case, remember?" Vegas reminded him.

"Ah, yes. How's the case going anyway?"

She admitted, "It's getting a little confusing at the moment. So far, two more deaths have taken place."

"Goodness," Pepper said in shock. "Were they killed over chess?"

"Don't know, but maybe I can find some information here. I've never been to a chess tournament before. Do they sell popcorn or anything?"

"No, you either play or watch. Or these days, text while pretending to watch."

They walked to the gymnasium where the tournament was being held when Vegas noticed a sign above the door that read Blue Falls Fighting Flying Flucos.

"What in the world is a Flying Fluco?" she asked.

"Their mascot. They changed the name from the Chiefs to the Flying Flucos a couple years ago," Pepper said.

Vegas again looked at the colorful sign. "I've never heard of a Flying Fluco. Is it a bird?"

"No, they made it up. They wanted a mascot that wouldn't offend anyone, and they came up with Flying Flucos."

"Was anybody offended by that?" Vegas asked.

"Oh, yeah."

They walked to a small table outside the gymnasium where two young men — one very skinny and the other a bit on the chunky side — were taking admission. They both had on suits that didn't fit them very well.

"Hey, Pepper. How are you doing?" asked the chunky one.

"I'm good."

"Who's the girl?" asked the skinny one.

"I'm Vegas."

"Are you into chess?" the big one asked.

"I'm just checking into it. Do you all play?"

They both got boastful looks on their faces, and the big one said, "Yeah, I play all the time. They call me the Falcon."

"Oh, well, that's ... odd," Vegas said.

"I don't have a nickname yet," the skinny one said. "I've been playing around with calling myself Cucumber because all of my moves make my opponents green with envy."

Vegas looked at him and then at Pepper. "Are you required to have a nickname that doesn't make any sense in order to play chess?"

"It's not required, it just makes it cooler," Pepper said.

"Do you have one?" she asked him.

"Well, they call me Serpent," he said, embarrassed.

"Is there a particular reason they call you that?"

"One time I wore a shirt with a serpent on it and won the tournament, so I became known as that. The name kind of stuck."

"Makes sense," Vegas said. She looked at the poster board duct-taped to the table. Scrawled on it with a black magic marker were the words "Admission: Five dollars for adults. Seven dollars for loud kids."

She started to unzip her purse when Pepper stopped her and said, "This is on me."

"Well, aren't you a gentleman," said Vegas, which

brought a hint of a blush from Pepper. "Thank you. But this still isn't a date," she added.

Pepper pointed toward his right temple with his index finger and said, "Up here, it's a date."

Pepper paid the ten dollars, and the two of them walked into the gym. People quieted and stared as they entered.

"It's quiet in here," Vegas said. "Has the tournament already started?"

"No, it's just that you're a pretty girl and they aren't used to that."

"Well, they know how to make a girl feel uncomfortable."

Soon people stopped gawking and started talking amongst themselves again.

Vegas and Pepper were walking around the room when a man in his fifties with graying temples came over to them.

"Hello, Pepper. I see you brought a girl," he said in a surprised voice.

"I'm just a friend," Vegas said.

"She's just a friend," added Pepper, then gave him a wink.

"I'm Bill Ward," he said to Vegas and shook her hand. "I run the tournament here. Will you be participating?"

"No, I'm new to chess," she said. "But when I heard a tournament would be held here at the Flying Flucos gymnasium, well, a girl couldn't stay away from that."

"I'm glad you came. I'm about to get things started. Pepper no doubt will tell you who to watch to pick up some strategies and techniques to incorporate into your game."

"I can't wait."

Pepper noticed a soda machine off to the side and asked, "Do you want a soda?"

"No, I'm good."

"I'm going to get one. It might help settle my nerves."

"What are you nervous about?" asked Vegas.

"I'm playing tonight and I don't want to lose, you know ... in front of you."

Vegas was touched. "You'll do fine."

"I hope so. I'll be right back."

Vegas stood alone for all of five seconds when a scrawny man in his mid-twenties walked over to Vegas with a cup of punch in each hand. He wore a red suit whose pants seemed several inches too short for him. He had on a white tie and Nike LeBron James shoes.

"Hello. I saw you were without any punch, so I brought you some. Of course, your beauty puts the punch in punch," he said in a leering voice.

"Oh, uh, no thank you," she said as she stared at the drink. "I didn't know they served punch here."

"I got it out of my car. I own a fifty-one Chevy. I'm hot-rodding it up now. All I need to do is replace the engine and keep the left front tire from falling off all the time."

"Yeah, keeping all your tires on is probably an important thing for hot-rodders."

"I'm Ronald McDonald," the man said with a smirk that irritated her considerably.

"Pardon?" asked a perplexed Vegas.

"I'm Ronald McDonald. I play chess."

"Oh. Are you any good?"

"I don't like to brag, but yes, I am. It's all in having a strong pawn center, as well as making sure you always move your knights before bishops. And be sure to castle early. I'll be happy to give you some private lessons if you wish?"

His smirk creeped her out and she said, "I'll pass, thank you."

"Maybe I could take you out and show you my car."

"No, I don't see that happening."

Strike two, Ronald thought and tried a new path to the pretty girl's heart. "I teach self-defense classes if you're interested. I'm into all the dangerous things."

"Were you in the military?"

"I was for a few days, but the drill sergeant made me leave. Said I was too extreme for them. But I've read all the books on being a sniper, bomb-making, fighting with your hands, that sort of thing."

"Sounds like you'd be a good terrorist."

"I'm into exotic pets, too. I owned an alligator for a while until he ate my neighbor. Well, almost ate him. I don't see why they blamed that on me anyway, it was a public pool."

Vegas willed him to leave, but he didn't get the message.

"You know, I'll be coming into a lot of money pretty soon. I'm getting into the real estate business. Thought I'd pass that on to you so you could be first in line," he said as he raised his eyebrows, which made him look like a disturbed Eugene Levy.

"I have to go speak to someone that isn't you," Vegas said and walked away.

He seemed surprised that she hadn't fallen for his best pickup lines but quickly moved on — he saw another woman in the crowd and immediately began his routine all over again.

Pepper rejoined Vegas as Bill Ward walked toward the front of the gym to start the tournament. Just then a shirt-less man dressed like a Mexican wrestler walked in. He had on a full mask, long black tights, black knee-high boots, and a black cape. Three very large men surrounded him as he walked through the room.

"Who, or maybe it would be better put, *what* was that?" Vegas asked in a whisper.

"That's The Ponderosa," Pepper informed her.

"The Ponderosa? Is he a big tree fan or something?" Vegas said.

"He's one of the best chess players in these parts, and he knows it. He's played several people at once, and he always wins."

"Does anybody know who he really is?" Vegas asked.

"There have been some good guesses, but no one really knows."

"Do you have any guesses?"

"I once thought he was Wilson Hopkins," Pepper said, "but I guess that's impossible now."

Vegas was taken aback by his comment but then turned her focus, along with everybody else, to Bill Ward, who was on stage holding a microphone.

"Attention everyone, attention. I'd like to welcome you all to the fourteenth edition of the Blue Falls Chess Masters Tournament brought to you by Ed's Septic Service. Their motto is 'We keep you going.' And they do, too," Ward added, which brought scattered laughter from the crowd.

"I'd also like to thank the Flying Flucos for providing the gymnasium for our tournament. It smells a lot better than the animal shelter we were at last year. Now, before we officially begin, I'm sure you all are aware that we lost one of our own recently: Wilson Hopkins passed away. His brother Bosco wanted to come tonight, but he said it was too soon. I think we all can understand that. So in honor of Wilson, I think it would be a good thing to observe a moment of silence in his memory."

Everyone was quiet as they all bowed their heads in silent prayer for their fallen comrade. Vegas thought it was touching.

Suddenly, a voice that sounded like it was coming from a radio called out, "This is Momma Bear to Baby Bear, come in, please."

A few people looked up, but most kept their heads bowed in respect for the moment.

Then the voice called out again. "Momma Bear to Baby Bear, come in, please."

This time when she heard it, there was no doubt in Vegas' mind that the voice belonged to her mother. But she wasn't sure where the voice was coming from. In an attempt to look around, Vegas glanced up while trying to keep her head bowed.

Then she heard it again. "Momma Bear to Baby Bear, come in. I know you can hear me, Vegas."

Vegas realized the voice was coming from inside her small purse. With a great deal of embarrassment, she hurried to the girls' locker room at the far end of the gym while trying to be invisible. Why was her mother always placing her in humiliating predicaments like this?

As she walked into the locker room, she heard Ward end the moment of silence by saying "Amen." Which was quickly followed by, "Did you hear a voice?"

Now safely deep in the locker room, Vegas opened her purse and found a walkie-talkie that her mother had obviously put there before she left for the evening.

"Mom, what do you want?" Vegas said as she pushed the call button on the radio.

"Well, it took you long enough to answer. Over," Eleanor called out.

"Everyone heard you in there — you called when we were having a moment of silence for Wilson Hopkins."

There was a moment of silence on Eleanor's end before she said, "Sounds like my timing may have been a little off. Over."

"Your timing is always off, and it's never by a little."

"Okay. Well, I have something important to say," Eleanor said.

Vegas waited for her to reply, but she remained silent. Vegas impatiently asked, "Mom, what's so important?"

"Wait a minute, Buttermilk wants to talk to you." There was a pause, then Eleanor added, "Over."

Vegas rolled her eyes as she heard strange sounds

coming from the speaker. Then she heard her mother say, "Don't lick it, talk to her."

"Buttermilk, put Mom back on," Vegas said.

"I'm Momma Bear," Eleanor called out. "You're Baby Bear. We have to use our code names so no one will know it's us. Over."

"Why did you put a radio in my purse?"

"For safety. That way if you need anything, you can radio me. Over."

"How could I have radioed you if I wasn't even aware that I had a walkie-talkie with me?"

"Hence my radio check just now! I think it worked flawlessly. Over," Eleanor replied.

Vegas took the radio and slowly banged it against her forehead as if she was punishing herself for being born into the family. Then Vegas asked, "Where exactly are you?"

"I'm outside behind a bush near the building. Over."

"You followed me?"

"You told me where you were going, Vegas. Over."

"I told you where I was going so you wouldn't worry, not so you could track me down."

"There's no need to get upset. Now, where are you exactly? Over."

"I'm in the girl's locker room."

"Is that this rectangle window that is above me here? Over."

Vegas looked around the room and saw a rectangular window made of privacy glass. She walked to it, opened it up, and stuck her head out the window. There she saw her mother and Buttermilk behind a bush.

Eleanor looked at her daughter and then said into her walkie-talkie, "Hi, honey. You look nice. Over."

"You need to go on back home."

"Did you get any leads?" Eleanor said through the radio. "Over."

"You don't have to talk through your radio now. I'm looking right at you."

"I know," Eleanor replied without using the radio. "It's just fun to use them. I think I found my inner seven-year-old boy with these things."

"Why are you here?"

"I'll tell you in a second. Do you think I can fit through this window?"

"You can't come through the window. You'll get hurt, plus they charge admission here. You'll get us both in trouble."

Eleanor ignored her daughter's advice and pulled herself onto the window sill. She grunted and groaned as she tried to get in, then suddenly stopped moving.

"Honey, I'm stuck."

Vegas sighed. "I can't believe you did this. How am I going to get you out?"

"I'm guessing lots of butter," Eleanor said.

"Lots of butter is why you won't fit through the window to begin with," Vegas said.

"It's almost like the window is giving birth to me. Push, window, push!" Eleanor said as she began twisting her body from side to side to try and ease her way into the locker room.

Vegas grabbed her mother by the wrists, placed her

right foot against the wall, then pulled hard until Eleanor popped free — and landed right on top of her daughter.

"We did it," Eleanor said. She sat up and looked around. "It's been a long time since I've been in a girl's locker room. Or boys, for that matter. The smell hasn't changed any though." Then she realized, "Speaking of smells, Buttermilk! I forgot him outside!"

"That dog probably ran away in embarrassment by now," Vegas mumbled.

Eleanor stood up, quickly walked over to the window, and looked out. "No, he doesn't really run away from anything. Or even move. Hi, boy! Mommy's okay."

Vegas got up and joined her mother at the window. "What are you going to do with him?"

"He'll be okay there. I'll go into the chess room with you to help you solve the case. I'll be your muscle."

Vegas looked at her mother and helped her fix her tousled hair as she said, "I don't understand you at all."

"It's called bonding," Eleanor said.

As the two of them walked out of the locker room, Vegas asked, "When did you put that radio in my purse?"

"When you came over to my house to take a shower. I got the radios because I saw them on sale and thought they could help us. And, boy, was I right. I also put a coupon in your purse for corn dogs. No matter how tired you are in life, you can always fix a corn dog to eat."

Vegas and her mother walked back into the gym and were met by a familiar face.

"Excuse me," said the man. "I think I've seen you two before."

"We met at Sergeant Miller's office," Vegas said. "You flushed your body camera down the toilet."

"Oh, yeah," he said, embarrassed. "I'm Officer Cody Perkins. Well, just Cody tonight."

"Were you fired?" Eleanor asked.

"No. The sergeant got me another camera, and I just had to pay half the cost. That's fair."

"Are you investigating something here?" Vegas asked, wondering if Sergeant Miller sent him.

"I was supposed to work tonight, but when I told the sergeant about the chess tournament, he let me have the night off. He told me to keep my radar up. I don't know what that means."

"Do you play chess?" asked Eleanor.

"I recently started playing. I used to play Scrabble, but I can't spell worth a lick, and that kind of hindered my game."

"I guess it would," Vegas said.

At that moment, three little people dressed like Abraham Lincoln walked in. No one in the room could take their eyes off of them.

"They look like an army of pennies marching off to the bank," Eleanor said.

"It looks like an episode of *The Twilight Zone* that needs a rewrite," Vegas added.

The three of them stared at the Lincoln impersonators as they made their way toward their group. Eleanor whispered, "What makes a man dress up like Abraham Lincoln in the first place?"

"Chicks," Cody answered.

"Chicks?" Vegas said.

The impersonators walked by them. Vegas stopped one of the men before he left and said, "Uh, excuse me, could I ask you something?"

"About what?"

"You're dressed like a new-age Pilgrim. What do you think I'm going to ask you?" Vegas asked.

"I just met you, so I don't know," the Lincoln impersonator said snippily. She clearly had offended him.

"Why are you all dressed up like Abraham Lincoln?"

"Because he's the greatest president we ever had."

"I think the Beatles were the greatest band of all time, but I don't go around dressing up like Ringo," Vegas said.

Eleanor interrupted. "One Halloween I dressed up as a beetle. The animal kind."

"Why?" Cody asked.

"I think they're cute. Much cuter than Ringo, at least," she replied.

Vegas shook her head and turned back to the Lincoln guy. "How do you get a job as a Lincoln impersonator?"

"We're not impersonators, we're educators."

"So you go to schools and such?" Eleanor asked.

"We opened up a mall today."

"A mall?" Vegas asked.

"It's a slow period for education right now. Now, if you'll excuse me, we're here to inspire the participants. I have to go. Goodbye," the educator said and walked away.

Vegas saw that the guy stopped to talk to Ronald McDonald. She took note of it.

A couple of minutes later, the games began. From

seven-thirty until one o'clock in the morning, chess matches were held nonstop, until there were only two contestants left: Pepper and The Ponderosa.

The championship game went on for about thirty minutes until The Ponderosa checkmated Pepper. In response, The Ponderosa stood on a table and growled and shouted. How annoying, Vegas and Eleanor both thought.

He was given a trophy, a coupon for forty percent off a car wash, and a check for thirty-four dollars and seventeen cents that couldn't be cashed until two weeks from Friday.

Eleanor turned to Vegas and said, "Thank God this is over. This has been the most boring night of my life. Let's go home."

"No, not yet," Vegas said.

"Why not? I need to get Buttermilk home."

"You can go on home."

"Where are you going?"

"I'm going to try and solve a riddle," Vegas said and walked out of the building.

18

Vegas exited the gym into the darkness. Most of the people were getting in their cars, but some were making casual conversation. Vegas looked around for The Ponderosa and finally spotted him getting in the back seat of a black Chevy Suburban parked across the street.

Vegas quickly made her way to her car and waited for the Suburban to leave. As she waited, Pepper came over and asked, "Did you like the tournament?"

"Uh, sure. I'm so sorry that you lost," Vegas said while trying to keep an eye on the Suburban without coming across as rude or letting Pepper know what she was doing.

"It was my own fault," Pepper said. "I always lose my concentration toward the end; my mind tends to wander. I got to thinking about the difference between turnips and radishes instead of focusing on the moves. I think it's because The Ponderosa takes so long between moves. I just get bored sitting there and then, boom, the great vegetable debate begins."

"Yeah, that happens to all of us, them vegetables and all," Vegas said distractedly. The Suburban began to pull away, and Vegas said hurriedly, "I gotta go, see you later." Pepper just stood there watching her leave and wondered what he had said to chase her away.

Vegas pulled out of the lot and followed the Suburban at what she figured was a safe distance. The Suburban traveled slowly along the streets, making a stop at a supermarket and then at a gas station to refuel. The Ponderosa sat in the back seat and didn't get out at either stop. Only the driver, a very large man, got out to do the task.

Vegas continued to follow the Suburban as it made a right turn onto the interstate. Vegas thought that anyone this popular in the chess world would know more than most about all the players. If he could afford a security team, he could also afford to do research on each opponent, learn their weaknesses and strengths. Odds were, she thought, that he either knew who might be the killer, or he was the killer himself.

The Suburban got off at the next exit and made a right turn, then a little farther on made a left into a warehouse parking lot. Vegas drove by and swung around to a rundown motel that was across from the warehouse, turned off her key, and sat in the darkness watching the Suburban.

The Suburban was idling in front of a garage door. The Ponderosa soon got out, still wearing his mask and outfit, and headed to the front of the warehouse with his three extraordinarily large friends. The men were talking and appeared to be waiting for someone.

A minute later, a car pulled into the warehouse parking lot, and The Ponderosa and his men walked to it. She couldn't make out what kind of vehicle this new car was, but she thought it was unusual-looking and probably an older model.

A person inside the car handed a package to The Ponderosa, and the car sped off. They got back in the Suburban and backed up. Vegas sank down into her seat as the Chevy's lights streaked across her car. Thank goodness The Ponderosa didn't know her car, she thought.

As the Suburban headed west, a vehicle parked directly behind Vegas' car. She froze. The car's headlights made it impossible to see. Was this the unusual-looking vehicle coming to start a fight? Did The Ponderosa send someone to attack her? Did she need to make a quick getaway? Vegas braced herself for anything.

The driver's door opened, and Vegas watched as a figure approached. She was too curious to just speed away, so she waited nervously for the person to reach her car.

"Hi, honey, I almost lost you," the person said.

Vegas was incredibly relieved and annoyed at the same time.

"I can't believe it's you!"

"It is. Surprise!" Eleanor said with a laugh.

"Would you be quiet? I'm on a case here."

"Sorry. To be honest, you look a bit disoriented. Like when you were little and you would spin around real fast until you fell down. Your father and I thought something might be wrong with you, but—"

"Mom," Vegas interrupted. "Can we talk about my childhood some other time?"

"Okay, honey, we'll set aside a night this week."

"No, that's not— Never mind. Why are you here? I thought you were going home."

"It's just that me and Buttermilk got worried about you when you left. I knew you were doing something about the case, and I don't see why you didn't tell me where you were going so I could help."

"Why didn't you just contact me with your walkie-talkie?"

"I lost it. I set it down somewhere in the gym, and I never did find the thing. Do you still have yours?"

"It's in my purse. Anyway, how did you find me?"

"Pepper pointed me in the direction you were going, and I got your scent pretty quickly. I'm getting really good at following people. I'd be a good car repo guy."

"Look into that tomorrow, why don't you? But now I have to go."

"Do I get in with you?" asked Eleanor.

"No, go on home. I need to try to find that Suburban and keep following it."

"That doesn't sound safe. I'll come with you. Let me get Buttermilk."

Eleanor started walking to her vehicle and Vegas yelled, "No, Mom. Just go home, and take that dog with you."

"That's not how a daughter should talk to her mother."

Suddenly a vehicle screeched into the motel parking lot and stopped abruptly beside Vegas and Eleanor. It was the Suburban. The three large men got out with guns pointed at them.

"Get in the car," grunted one of the men.

"Thank you, but we have rides," Eleanor said.

"Mom, I don't think they're asking."

"Well, I'm not going without Buttermilk," Eleanor said.

"Lady, I'm not stopping to get you a carton of buttermilk," one of the men said.

"Buttermilk is my dog," she said and went to her SUV and grabbed the pooch. She walked back to the gunmen.

Vegas stared at her mother. "Why didn't you make a run for it just now?"

"Oh, I couldn't leave you all alone with gun guys. Besides, you might need me to help you fight them," Eleanor said.

Vegas shook her head as her mother asked one of the men, "Could you point that gun in another direction? When guns are pointed at me it makes me nervous, and when I get nervous I talk a lot."

"She'll talk a lot if you point spoons at her," Vegas said.

"I don't think that was necessary," Eleanor said. "If we're going to be business partners, we need to talk nice about each other in front of evil villains."

"We don't know that they're—"

One of the men interrupted, "Is this your mother?"

"Yes," Vegas said.

"You shouldn't be talking to her like that then," he said. "I mean, you only get one mom."

"That's right," Eleanor said with a nod of her head.

"All right, enough family time — get in the Suburban," another gunman said.

Vegas didn't want to do that if she could help it, so she did the first thing that came to mind and shouted, "Run, Mom, run!"

The gunmen watched placidly as Eleanor slowly ran around Vegas' car and squatted behind it. Vegas rolled her eyes and asked, "Mom, what are you doing?"

"Shh," Eleanor whispered.

One of the men looked at Vegas and asked, "What's she doing?"

"I have no idea. Ask her yourself."

"Ma'am, why are you hiding behind the car?"

Eleanor rose up with her hands in the air and said, "Vegas said run, but I didn't know where to go, so I just ran behind the car."

"Well, get back here," he growled.

Eleanor came back and stood beside Vegas. Then, spying Buttermilk at their feet, tried a new approach.

"You all had better watch out because I've got an attack dog," Eleanor threatened. "He's got a vicious demeanor. Get 'em, boy!"

Buttermilk looked at Eleanor and then walked over to the Suburban and attempted to get into the opened door, but he failed to and just plopped down and closed his eyes.

"Uh, one of you is going to have to help him up, and then, watch out!" Eleanor said.

One of the men patted Buttermilk behind the ears, then picked him up and placed him in the cargo area of the Suburban. The other two men lowered their guns and placed handcuffs on Vegas and Eleanor.

"See why I didn't want you to come with me, Mom?"

"Yep, I see it now," Eleanor said, nodding. She then pleaded with the men, "Please just let her go. I'll be your hostage."

"You're not a hostage," one of the men said.

"Why are you handcuffing us if we're not hostages?" asked Vegas.

"So you don't get away. Now be quiet, we have some questions for you."

"How can we answer your questions if we're being quiet?" Eleanor asked.

"And first, I have some questions for your boss," Vegas said. "Like where is he?"

"Yeah, I have questions, too," Eleanor added. "Namely, where did he get these handcuffs? Was it a two-for-one sale or something? They itch like crazy."

"Get the tape," said the man who seemed like the leader.

"Why do you want tape?" asked Eleanor.

"So you two will shut up," he said.

One of the men threw him a roll of duct tape. He tore off a piece and placed it over Eleanor's mouth.

"I have to admit, I've often fantasized about someone duct taping my mother's mouth," Vegas said.

He tore a second piece off and placed it over Vegas'

mouth. He directed the pair into the back of the Suburban with Buttermilk, whose mouth they didn't duct tape, Eleanor noted with satisfaction. He could call for help when the time came, she thought.

19

After thirty minutes of what seemed like aimless driving up avenues and down side streets, the Suburban finally stopped. The three men got out and left Vegas and Eleanor lying down in the cargo area with Buttermilk. When Vegas thought the men were out of sight, she rose up slowly and looked out the window.

There was nobody around, so she got on her knees and started rubbing her face against the back of the seat in an attempt to get the duct tape off her mouth. After a few attempts, she managed to get it off her lips, though it still dangled from her cheek.

"Are you okay, Mom?" Vegas said.

Eleanor tried talking through the tape but couldn't make herself understood.

"Now will you listen to me when I tell you that I don't want you to come with me on any of these cases?"

Eleanor nodded yes.

"I told you this was dangerous, but you wouldn't believe me. You believe me now, right?"

Eleanor again nodded yes.

"See if you can get the tape off like I did," Vegas said.

Eleanor wobbled back and forth like a child's toy as she tried to get up. Finally, she got on her knees and began rubbing her face up against the back of the seat the way she saw Vegas do it. After several tries, then several more, the tape began to peel off enough to where she could talk.

"Oh, my goodness, that's the longest I've gone without talking in my life," Eleanor gasped.

Vegas looked around outside again and realized she knew where they were.

"We're back at the warehouse. Why would they make us lay down in the back of a Suburban, handcuff us, put duct tape on our mouths, drive all over town, then simply take us across the street from where all of this began?"

"They sound indecisive," Eleanor said.

"What?"

"They were probably going to take us somewhere else, then decided that wouldn't work because that's where we would expect them to take us, so then they had to bring us here instead. And then get Louis, too."

"Who in the world in Louis?"

"All bad guys are named Louis," Eleanor said.

Vegas stared at her mother and then said, "Mom, put your tape back on."

Vegas examined the warehouse. There was a window visible near the front and a light on inside, but she couldn't see anything but what appeared to be a hallway.

"When I was across the street watching them before you came and scared me to death, I saw a car stop out front here. Someone inside handed the big guys a package."

"What was in it?" asked Eleanor.

"I don't know. It was a box of some kind."

"Why would they give them a box?"

"I don't know," Vegas said in frustration. "But I do know there's something wrong with a chess champion who wears a mask and kidnaps people."

Eleanor thought it over and said, "Well, in his defense, you were following him."

"That doesn't give you a right to handcuff people and tape their mouths shut. Otherwise, I would have done that to you a long time ago," Vegas said.

Eleanor ignored her remark and asked, "How can we get these cuffs off?"

"I don't know."

"Oh, I know what we could do," Eleanor said. "I saw it one time on a TV show. These people escaped out the window from a house, and they put their shoes on the wrong feet so the bad guys wouldn't know which direction they went."

"How does putting your shoes on the wrong feet trick anybody about which direction you went?" Vegas asked.

"Because the footprints are backward."

"But they're still pointing in the direction you are going," Vegas said.

Eleanor became frustrated. "It'll come to you if you just think it through."

"Did this TV show happen to be a cartoon?"

Eleanor sighed in frustration and pledged to be silent as a punishment, but that lasted all of five seconds.

"Do you see any clues?" Eleanor asked when she noticed Vegas staring at the warehouse window.

"Just a hallway. I keep hoping to see somebody walk by."

"Hey, maybe Buttermilk can bite off our handcuffs," Eleanor suggested.

"He can't bite through metal," Vegas said. "He's not a superpowered dog, for crying out loud."

"Well, I'm new at being kidnapped. I'm open to any ideas here."

Suddenly the warehouse door opened, and the three large men exited. They walked to the Suburban and opened the back.

"Hey, your tape is off," said one of the men.

"A woman's gotta talk," Eleanor said.

The man scowled and helped Vegas and Eleanor out of the vehicle. The men then started to lead the duo away when Eleanor pushed her way back to the Suburban and scooped up Buttermilk. The ladies were led to the warehouse, and everyone in the group — five humans and one canine — entered and walked down the hallway that Vegas had seen through the window. They were shown to a small office on the left.

One of the men sat behind a large desk in the center of the room, while the other two brought Vegas and Eleanor to their seats: ladder-back chairs that faced the desk. Vegas looked up at a Mickey Mouse clock on the wall. It read two twenty-five a.m. Her eyes danced over to a box behind the man on a table. She was positive this was the package that she saw delivered to them earlier.

"Why are you following our client?" asked the man behind the desk.

"What makes you think I'm following anybody? I was just outside arguing with my mother," Vegas said.

"I wouldn't call it arguing," Eleanor replied. "It's just that I worry about her all the time. She doesn't have a husband, and I don't want her to end up alone. Are any of you single?"

"Mom!" screamed Vegas. "I'm not going to date someone who kidnapped me."

"We didn't kidnap you," the man behind the desk said.

"You put handcuffs on us, put duct tape over our mouths, shoved us into a vehicle, and took off. That sounds like a kidnapping to me," Vegas said.

"It wasn't a kidnapping," the man said. "All we were doing was trying to secure a threat."

"What threat?" Eleanor asked.

"You two."

"We aren't a threat," Vegas said. "I admit that we're a little strange, but we aren't a threat."

"We have to protect our client," the man said. "That's what we're paid to do, and that's what I'm going to do. You two could have had bombs on, for all I know."

"I'm not wearing a bomb, I'm just naturally chunky," Eleanor said huffily.

"Who is your client?" Vegas asked.

"The Ponderosa."

"I mean, what's his real name?" she asked.

"That's all you need to know," the man said sternly.

"Why does he have a security team? Does he get a lot of threats?"

"He's cautious is all. Now, why were you following him?"

"I'm curious about who he is," Vegas responded.

"Why do you want to know that?"

"He has a mask on and he wins chess tournaments — everybody wants to know who he is. I thought I'd try and find out. What's the big deal about that? And actually, I'm sure he wears a mask to create intrigue, so in a way, I'm just helping him with that."

At this point, Eleanor passed along a life experience.

"I went to school with a kid who wore a superhero mask in the first grade. He also had a stick horse. Or was it a magic broom? I think it changed every day. ... To be brutally honest, I don't think he was all there. He wore a superhero mask to school, after all."

"What are your names?" the man behind the desk said.

"You tell us your names first," Vegas said.

"I'm Eleanor."

"Don't tell him your name, Mom," Vegas scolded.

"But he asked," Eleanor said defensively.

The man looked at Vegas and asked, "So this woman is your mother?"

"How do you know that?" Vegas asked.

"You just called her Mom."

Vegas got a "doggone it, I messed up" look on her face.

Eleanor tried to fix the situation. "My real name is actually Quinby Bartles."

Vegas looked at her mother, and Eleanor gave her a little wink to say she had it all under control.

The man behind the desk tried to get the conversation back on track. "The Ponderosa doesn't want you following him anymore. Who he is is his business and no one else's. Do you two understand that?"

"Sure," Vegas said. "By the way, what's the name of your security team?"

"None of your business."

Eleanor quickly chimed in, "I think I could have come up with a better name than None of Your Business."

"That's not the name of our— Oh, never mind," the man behind the desk said in frustration.

"I don't think you're a real security team," Vegas said.

"Yeah, where are your badges and hats?" asked Eleanor.

The man paused for a moment and said, "We're undercover security."

"Like the Secret Service," said the man behind Vegas.

"I'm thinking you're more like bouncers at a nightclub that are trying to make extra money at night. Is that what it is?" Vegas asked confidently.

"That's none of your business," the man behind the desk said.

"I believe a real security team would have called the police by now," Vegas said. "They wouldn't have taken us to a warehouse in handcuffs and duct taped our mouths shut. But you can't call the police because they would probably know who you are. I'm sure you've got a police record of some kind. Right? So now you need to let us go immediately, or there's going to be problems for everyone here."

The man behind the desk thought it over and said, "Go ahead and take the cuffs off."

Vegas and Eleanor stood up, and the men behind them unlocked their cuffs. The women rubbed their wrists to get the feeling back in them.

"Are we free to go now?" Vegas asked. She looked again at the box behind the desk.

"You're free to go. Don't follow our client ever again. As long as you do that, we shouldn't have any trouble with you," the man behind the desk said.

"I certainly won't follow him anymore," Eleanor said, then quickly moved on. "By the way, I'm afraid that my dog may have gone potty in the back of your vehicle."

"What?" the man behind the desk said.

"Well, he scares easily," Eleanor said. "I mean, seeing your mother and sister handcuffed before your eyes is quite troubling."

"Buttermilk isn't my brother," Vegas said.

"Shh, he'll hear you," scolded Eleanor as she looked to see if Buttermilk had taken offense. "Where is he? My baby's gone! Don't worry, Buttermilk, Mommy's coming!"

Eleanor ran out of the office yelling for her dog.

Vegas quickly followed and joined the search. The three men, eager to get these two crazy women out of their lives, even helped.

"Maybe he went upstairs," one of the men said.

Before Eleanor could tell him that wasn't possible,

Vegas said, "Yes, he's always climbing stairs. Go up there and look."

"Vegas, he doesn't climb anything because—"

Vegas interrupted her and gave her a look. "Mom, I think I know my own brother. I'm sure he's upstairs. Could you strong men go look for him?"

The three men hurried up the stairs, and Eleanor began to explain why Buttermilk couldn't climb when Vegas shushed her and said, "No time. I'm going to the office. Holler if the guys come back down."

"Holler what?" Eleanor asked.

"Whatever. Just let me know when they're coming back," she said over her shoulder.

"I could shout 'Dupree,'" Eleanor said.

Vegas stopped. "Why?"

"It sounds cool. It sounds like something a TV detective would say."

"I don't need you yelling out cool names, just let me know when you see them coming down."

"I guess I should come up with a silent signal. Something universal," Eleanor said.

"A silent universal signal? That leaves mooning," Vegas said and took off down the hallway.

"Well, I'm not going to do that," Eleanor said with a blush.

Vegas ran into the office and headed straight for the package behind the desk. She carefully opened it and pulled out a solid-gold chess king. She then took out a solid-silver king. They seem genuine, she thought before putting them back in the box. As she put the box away, she noticed a leash by her foot. She bent down and saw Buttermilk sound asleep under the desk.

Outside the office, Eleanor heard the men coming down the stairs. She looked toward the office and whispered, "Dupree, Dupree."

Vegas didn't come out, and the men were on the first floor. Vegas was going to get caught if Eleanor didn't do something, so she did the first thing that came to mind: Use seduction. She placed her hand up on a door frame like a pinup model and smiled at the three men. "So, we're alone," she said with a smile and a wink.

Vegas exited the office, which put a stop to the dance Eleanor was about to do.

"Hey, you found Buttermilk!" she said.

"He was asleep under the desk."

Vegas then turned to the men, "We found him, thank you. We'll see ourselves out."

The men nodded, and Eleanor and Vegas headed toward the exit with Buttermilk.

"Did you find anything?"Eleanor asked.

"I'm not sure. It could be something."

They left the warehouse and noticed blinking lights across the street. Their vehicles were being towed away.

20

A t four o'clock in the morning, Vegas, Eleanor, and Buttermilk stumbled into Vegas' Airstream. Eleanor and Vegas looked as exhausted as they felt. They had spent the past hour negotiating with the tow truck driver, who didn't speak much English and had very little common sense, they thought. Eventually, they got their vehicles, however.

"I've never been so tired in all of my life," Eleanor said as she laid down on the bed.

"Yeah, it's been a long night, all right," Vegas replied, rubbing her eyes.

"Did you get a new ceiling?" Eleanor asked.

"What?"

"Did you get a new ceiling?"

"No, that's the ceiling it came with," Vegas said.

"I thought it was white."

"It is white."

"I'm so tired I can't even tell my colors apart anymore,"

Eleanor said, sitting up. "The last time I was this tired, it was because of that squirrel."

"What squirrel?" Vegas asked.

"I was cleaning when an evil squirrel came through the window and chased me all over the house. It was an odd day."

Vegas was too tired to respond to the strange story. They both sat motionless with their eyes slowly closing when Eleanor looked down at her dog and said, "I think Buttermilk is already asleep."

"He's been asleep for most of the time I've known him," Vegas said.

"Maybe all this sleep will help his legs grow," Eleanor said.

Vegas looked at her mother and asked, "Do you want to bunk here for the night?"

Eleanor's eyes shot open. "You want me to stay with you?"

"Just for tonight only. I don't want you driving when you're so tired. It wouldn't be safe."

"They say driving when you're tired is the same as driving after drinking thirty-five martinis."

"Thirty-five?"

"Not that I tried that, of course."

"So you're staying the night, or what's left of it?" Vegas asked.

"Are you sure you want me to? It's just I'm not used to you wanting me around. Lately, you've been wanting me to leave you alone."

"For safety reasons I've been wanting you to leave me

alone. After tonight you can see why. And now for safety reasons, I want you to sleep here."

"I knew your job had risks," Eleanor said. "After all, I've seen many detective TV shows. I guess I just didn't know the risks were quite this, well, risky."

Eleanor got up and Vegas prepared the bed. When it was ready, Eleanor let herself fall onto the bed, but this time she hit her head on the side of the camper.

"Ow," Eleanor managed to utter.

"Are you okay, Mom?"

Eleanor said nothing.

"Mom, did you knock yourself out?"

"I'm okay, sweetie," she groaned. "I'm not used to a wall being there."

Eleanor rolled over to make room, and Vegas laid down beside her.

"You know, it's been a long time since I've slept in this camper," Eleanor said. "The last time I was in it, your father took us on that fishing trip to the mountains. How old were you?"

"I think eight or nine. It was a big adventure for me to be in a camper, even if it was with my parents."

"You slept in a sleeping bag on the floor, and your father got up in the middle of the night and stepped on you. Ooo, you screamed like a crazy person! You scared us both half to death. We thought a bear was eating you."

"It scared me, too! I thought it was Bigfoot trying to grab me."

They were quiet for a few moments.

"They were good times," Eleanor said.

"It seems just like yesterday though, doesn't it?" Vegas said with a smile.

"Yeah, time kind of gets away from you after a while. One day your baby is standing in the middle of the creek shouting, 'I'm a purple monster!' Then the next day she's out solving crimes."

"Man, I was a strange kid," Vegas said. "Wasn't the last time we went camping that time that Dad caught a cow in the river?"

They both laughed.

"I have to admit that it was a bit startling to come out of the camper and see a cow in the river staring at me," Eleanor reminisced. "I mean, there was no way I was going to be able to cook that cow on that little stove over there."

Eleanor snorted with laughter, which made them both start laughing hysterically.

After a minute, Vegas asked, "Where did it even come from? There weren't any farms up in that part of the mountains. It was all woods."

"I guess cows do what cows do," replied Eleanor. "I didn't want to scare you at the time, but it could have been a ghost cow."

"No, it was a real cow — I stepped in its proof," Vegas said.

"Oh, well, I feel better now. Did you clean your feet before you came back into the camper?"

"I did the best I could."

They were quiet before Eleanor said, "I always hated camping."

"I didn't know that. You seemed to always love it when

I was little. We'd go several times a year, for a while anyway."

"I got tired of it. The bugs, the dirt, everything. I told your father that I wasn't a camping person anymore, so he parked the camper in the back until you moved out and took it. I especially hated the tiny bathroom. I prefer to be more comfortable when I go."

"That's an interesting comment considering your bathroom incident the other day."

They both laughed.

"I'd like to forget about that," Eleanor said.

The quietness surrounded them, filling both with peace. Eleanor volunteered, "The only reason I seemed to love camping is because I was with you and your father. I didn't love camping at all. It made no sense to me to leave a perfectly good house, hook this thing up to the truck, and drive up in the mountains to spend a weekend in an object that wasn't any bigger than one of your dollhouses."

"I loved my dollhouses," Vegas recalled. "I made a family out of clothespins and cut up some pillowcases for clothes and painted little faces on them. I called them Willie and Bertha Trucker."

Eleanor laughed. "How did you come up with those names?"

"Who knows. And their twin kids were called Tiger and Cinnamon. They were six years old because that's how old I was."

Eleanor's mind began to track through their past and she said, "I remember when we got you a Barbie and Ken doll for Christmas. You never played with Barbie, though, only Ken."

"I didn't call him Ken. I called him Thor Outlaw."

"Thor Outlaw?" repeated Eleanor.

"That was my goal in life, to meet a guy named Thor Outlaw. He'd be—" She paused, smiling at the memory. "Well, he'd be Thor Outlaw."

"I wouldn't approve of you dating a boy named Thor Outlaw. I'd worry myself to death about what he might get you into."

"You and I were just handcuffed in the back of a Suburban," Vegas said. "I think if I can handle that, I could handle Thor Outlaw."

"Yeah, but I'm sure Thor Outlaw would have had some other ideas, too."

Vegas smiled. "Yeah, I bet he would."

"Let's try and get some sleep now," Eleanor said, settling in.

"All right, goodnight," Vegas replied.

The exhaustion of the night's events began to take its effect, and they were about to fall asleep when they suddenly heard snoring. They sat up at the same time and looked at Buttermilk.

"Is he making all that noise?" Vegas asked.

"Yeah, that's my baby. He snores worse than I do. Maybe I should get him one of those masks to put on at night."

The two of them laid back down, and Buttermilk's snoring slowly faded away, when the payphone outside rang.

Eleanor rose up in a panic and looked down at Buttermilk. "Oh, my God, he's swallowed a bell!"

"It's the payphone," Vegas said as she scrambled to her feet and hurried outside to answer it.

She opened the door and immediately fell.

"I thought I heard something fall!" shouted Eleanor.

Vegas lay on the ground and could see the half moon glaring down at her from the black sky before shouting back to her mother, "That was just me!"

"Are you okay?"

"Eventually," Vegas replied as she got back on her feet. She hurried to the phone, picked it up, and it slipped right out of her hand. The telephone swung wildly from side to side before she was able to wrangle it back into her hand.

"Hello?" asked Vegas.

"Vegas?"

"Yeah. Who is this?"

"Are you fighting someone? You sound out of breath."

"No, I'm just a little tired, is all. Who is this?"

"It's me, Bosco Hopkins. I think I may have found something that will prove my brother was killed. Be at my apartment at seven."

"Seven?" Vegas asked. She thought seven seemed a little early for someone who felt dead.

"What time is it now?"

"It's a little after four," Bosco replied.

"Why are you calling me now?"

"I've been calling you all day, but I couldn't get anybody to answer. Did you turn your cellphone off or something?"

"Uh, no, it's in the shop getting its oil changed," Vegas said, embarrassed by the fact that she couldn't afford a cellphone.

"Oil changed?" asked Bosco. There was a short pause followed by, "Do you have the Black iPhone ?"

"I, uh, yeah, yeah. The Alien Five."

"They do exist," Bosco whispered.

"How about we meet at noon?" Vegas asked.

Bosco suggested, "How about nine?"

"Ten," Vegas said.

"Nine-thirty," countered Bosco. "Meet me at my place. Apartment thirty. It's right above Wilson's."

"Sold," Vegas said and hung up, then headed back into the camper and collapsed in exhaustion, and fell asleep somewhere between the bed and the snoring dog.

21

Vegas woke up. Her eyes were trying to persuade her to go back to sleep when the sound of a vehicle starting jarred her into action. She sat up, still confused with sleepiness, and glanced at her Popeye alarm clock. Nine o'clock.

"I'm late," Vegas blurted out as she scrambled to her feet. She grabbed her things and looked out the window. There she saw her mother trying to start the SUV.

Vegas went outside, hurried over to her mother's vehicle, and asked, "Are you trying to escape?"

"I was going to go and get us something to eat, but the vehicle won't start."

"Does it have any gas?"

"Of course it has gas," Eleanor said. "I wouldn't run the vehicle out of gas. Your father taught me better than that."

Vegas stuck her head through the opened driver's-side window, turned the key on, and looked at the gas gauge. It was on E.

"Mom, it's out of gas."

Eleanor looked like she was trying to invent a new type of fuel on the spot. All she could come up with was, "Maybe we could run it off french fry grease."

"No, Mom. Besides, I don't have any french fry grease."

"I saw some people do it on TV one time. They went to a fast-food place and asked for their grease, and they seemed more than happy to give it away. So it wouldn't cost us anything."

"Mom, this is a gasoline engine. If you pour grease down there, you'll plug it up and destroy it all."

"Then what do we do?"

"We go and get you some gas to put in it."

"But it's out of gas. ... Oh, you mean go get some gas in your car, then bring it back here?" Eleanor said.

"Yeah, but I have to go to an appointment right now. I'm already late."

"Appointment with who?"

"Bosco. He was the one who called last night. He thinks he might have some information for me about his brother's death."

"I'll come with you."

"You can stay here."

"What am I going to do here?"

"You can clean the place up," Vegas said as she headed to her car.

Eleanor looked at the camper and shook her head. "I'm not going to clean this place. Why on Earth would I try to make it look nice for you? I want you to move out of here."

Eleanor got out of her vehicle, opened the back door,

and pulled out Buttermilk who, as usual, was sound asleep. She hurried to Vegas' car, opened the passenger-side door, and got in.

"Why are you coming with me? You need to stay here and get some sleep."

"I'm wide awake. Buttermilk sleeps enough for both of us. Oh, do you have a gas can?"

"No."

"Milk jugs?"

"No."

"Why wouldn't you have any milk jugs? I thought everybody had milk jugs. Don't you drink milk?" asked Vegas' perplexed mother.

"No, I drink coffee and water."

Eleanor stared at her daughter and shook her head. "I can't believe what you're telling me right now."

"Why? I like coffee and water. What's the big deal? It's one of the basic food groups."

"You need to drink milk to build up your bones. Do you want soft bones?"

"I get my calcium through breakfast bars," Vegas said as she started her car.

"How am I going to get any gas if I don't have anything to put it in?"

"We'll pick up a jug of milk on the way back," Vegas said as she sped out of the campground toward the Rhinehouse Apartments as fast as she dared. They arrived late, and Vegas quickly got out and headed toward the front entrance when she heard her mother call out to her, "Vegas, I'm stuck!"

Vegas turned and saw that Buttermilk's leash had got tangled up in the car's shoulder belt.

"How do you manage to get his leash tangled up in everything?" asked an upset Vegas.

"I don't know. I guess I'm not good with technology," Eleanor said.

After Vegas got the two untangled, they hurried to Bosco's apartment. Vegas knocked on the door and waited.

"I can't believe I'm late again," she said. "Seems like I'm always late these days."

"I'm never late," Eleanor said.

"What do you mean you're never late? You're the main reason I'm always late in the first place. Also, why does Buttermilk have to go everywhere with us?"

"He needs the mental stimulation of fighting crime. Lord knows he doesn't get much physical stimulation."

Bosco opened the door and peeked over the chain lock at them. He stared at them without saying a word.

"What's the information you have for me?" Vegas asked.

Bosco still didn't say anything.

"Can we come in?" Vegas tried again.

Again, Bosco didn't say anything or move. He just stared at them.

Eleanor grabbed Vegas by the arm, pulled her away from the door, and whispered, "Do you think someone is in the apartment with him and has a gun on him?"

"I don't know. He could be trying to hypnotize us, for all I know. He's a strange—" Vegas stopped. She realized what he wanted.

She stood in front of his door and said, "Rumpel-stiltskin."

Bosco opened the door.

Vegas shrugged at Eleanor, and they entered the apartment. Bosco closed the door behind them.

"You said on the phone that you found something that would prove your brother was murdered," Vegas said.

"I did," replied Bosco as he stared blankly at Vegas.

"Hello?" Vegas said after a moment of silence.

Eleanor tried to help by saying, "Rumpelstiltskin."

"What?" Bosco asked.

"What's the information?" asked a frustrated Vegas.

"Oh, you want to know now?"

"Uh, yes."

"So I went to my brother's storage locker yesterday to retrieve all of his things. When I got there, it had his rings, cash, his comic book collection, clothes, his toys—"

"Toys?" Eleanor interrupted. "He played with toys in a storage locker?"

"You don't play with toys! That would devalue them," a horrified Bosco said. "But I did notice that one thing was missing."

"What?" prodded Vegas.

"Let me guess," Eleanor said.

"No, we're not playing a game here," Vegas said.

"I don't mind letting her guess," Bosco said.

"Was it a dog?" Eleanor asked.

"In a storage locker?" Vegas said in an irritated voice.

"Oh, that's right. Hmm. Was it a chess set?"

Bosco looked at Eleanor with his mouth agape. "Oh, my God," he practically shouted. "You're a psychic."

"I got it right?" asked an excited Eleanor. She turned to Vegas and told her, "I always had a feeling someday I would have psychic abilities."

Vegas rolled her eyes, then addressed Bosco. "Was it a special set or something?"

"Yes," Bosco said. "He won it in a chess match in Europe. It was worth a million dollars. It was rumored to have once been owned by Napoleon Bonaparte. He was the leader of France at one time. Well, actually twice."

"We know who Napoleon is," Vegas said.

"I love his ice cream," Eleanor said.

"Okay, one of us knows who Napoleon is," Vegas added.

Vegas paused, thinking deeply, then asked, "This chess set, were the pieces made of gold and silver?"

Bosco's jaw dropped again. "You're psychic, too!"

"Yay," Eleanor said as she clapped her hands softly together. "We should go on the *Price is Right* together. We'll make a fortune. Actually, we should try to make a fortune on *Wheel of Fortune*. That would be more appropriate."

Vegas ignored her mother and told Bosco, "I saw this chess set. It was in the warehouse where the security team held us."

"Security team?" Bosco asked. "What do you mean? You were arrested?"

"Not exactly," Eleanor said. "Or were we arrested? I'm

not sure. I guess that's a sign that they didn't do it right. Or that I need to pay more attention."

"They were an overzealous security team," Vegas said. "They taped our mouths shut, handcuffed us, and put us in the back of a Suburban. Then they took us to the warehouse."

Bosco had a terrified look on his face as he paced the room. "This is getting too dangerous. I don't want anything to happen to the two of you."

He stopped pacing and looked at Vegas. "I've grown ... very fond of you. You could be my wife one day."

"I'll never be your wife," Vegas said quickly.

"I'm calling this whole thing off," Bosco said.

"You can't call it off," Eleanor said. "She doesn't have any other cases or husband prospects lined up."

"Mom!" shouted Vegas. "You can't call it off now — I know where the chess set is! Or where it was."

"But I don't want anyone else to die," Bosco said as he went over to an extra-large rocking horse that he had in the corner of the room, got on it, and began rocking back and forth. Eleanor and Vegas stared at each other in alarm.

"Dear God, what's he doing?" Eleanor whispered to Vegas.

"I'm not sure, but I don't think he's going to get away," Vegas said. "Maybe this is the way he deals with stress."

"When you were little and stressed out, you used to put rocks up your nose," Eleanor said.

"That didn't have anything to do with stress. I was just another dumb little kid."

"Your father thought it meant you weren't getting enough vitamins."

"Let's talk about the strangeness that I inherited from you some other time, okay?" asked Vegas.

Vegas walked over to Bosco. He appeared to be using the horse to calm himself down.

"I appreciate your worrying about me and my mother," Vegas began.

"The dog, too!" Bosco said.

"Yes, Buttermilk is appreciative, too," Vegas continued. "But you hired us because you thought somebody killed your brother. You want to know the truth, and I do, too. And I'm close to getting answers."

Bosco visibly calmed and stopped rocking. He then grabbed his wrist to check his pulse.

"Where did you get this rocking horse?" Eleanor asked.

"It was my brother's."

"That's sweet," she said. "I had one when I was little, but it kept falling over because I was a very aggressive hopper. The front of it would come off the floor, and the next thing I knew it would be laying on top of me. My mother would come in and shout, 'What is wrong with you?' And I just giggled."

"Mom," Vegas said as she placed her hand on her mother's arm to get her to stop talking.

Bosco said, "Wilson bought it off the internet. It was kind of a gag gift, you know. He didn't try to ride it to town or anything."

"Uh, right. Well, we all like to get some goofy things

every now and then," Vegas said. "Do you think it reminded him of his youth?"

"Yeah. We had a pony when we were smaller. We called him Jaws," Bosco said.

Vegas wondered aloud, "Why Jaws?"

"We were fans of the movie."

Eleanor turned to Vegas and asked, "Is that the one where the horse could talk?"

"No, it was about a killer shark. They're sorta like horses, I guess," Vegas replied.

"He only had three legs," Bosco said.

"A shark had three legs?" Eleanor asked.

"The pony," Bosco and Vegas said in unison.

"Oh, okay," Eleanor said. "I got lost in the conversation for a moment."

"Why did your pony only have three legs?" Vegas asked.

"He came that way."

"Your parents bought a pony with three legs?" Vegas said.

"Dad didn't realize he only had three legs. Though he did wonder why the sellers wouldn't allow him to walk around the pony before he bought it. But he was distracted a lot. So was my mom. Work kept them busy."

"What kind of work did they do?" Vegas asked.

"Dad was a gynecologist and Mom worked at the courthouse."

"Courthouse?" Vegas said, her mind turning. "Can she look something up for me?"

"I'm afraid she's dead. Both of my parents died a few years ago."

Vegas felt bad. Bosco looked upset again.

"I'm sorry," she said. "I was just wanting to check the deed to the warehouse and see who owns it."

"I can do it for you," Bosco said. "I have a computer. And a robot."

Vegas didn't understand the purpose of him telling her that he owned a robot, but she didn't understand him in general. And now he was on his knees in front of the couch. He reached under it and pulled out a box.

He opened it up and showed them pieces of a robot that looked like they had been through a wringer. They were thoroughly broken and covered in dirt and grass stains.

"Are you sure that's a robot?" Eleanor asked with a look she hadn't used since she saw a two-headed cow at the state fair.

"Oh, yeah, it's a robot, all right. It even flew," he said.

"Is it a drone?" Vegas asked.

"More like a rock. It has no aerodynamic shape to it. It did have wings, though. I made sure to add wings. I called it Floyd."

"Floyd?" asked Eleanor. "Does Floyd stand for anything?"

"Flying Robot," Bosco replied.

Vegas and Eleanor confusedly pondered the name for a moment. Then Bosco went on. "I belong to a drone club, and I wanted to make my own, so I built this. I have another one in the works that's much better than this one. It should be ready to test fly pretty soon."

"Well, can you check on the deed for me now?" asked Vegas.

"Oh, sure."

Bosco slid his robot back under the couch, got his laptop off the side table, sat down on the couch, and began punching the keys.

"Okay, I'm in," he said seconds later.

"That was fast," Vegas said, impressed. "Look up the warehouse on Sixth Avenue. The number on the building was three two eight."

"How did you see the warehouse number?" Eleanor asked.

"Mom, they put tape on our mouths, not our eyes."

Bosco quickly punched some more keys and said, "Frisco Jones owns it."

Vegas and Eleanor stared at each other.

"He owns the apartment building," Vegas said, trying to make sense of it. "And also the warehouse where I saw Wilson's chess set. What does that mean? ... Have you ever met Frisco Jones?"

Bosco thought for a moment and replied, "No, I don't think so."

"What about your rent?" Vegas said. "Where do you send it?"

"The security guard comes by at the first of the month and I give it to him," Bosco informed them.

"The security guard? That seems odd."

"That's the way I've always done it. Wilson did, too."

"Does everyone in the building pay their rent that way?" asked Vegas.

"As far as I know."

"Did you crack the case, honey?" Eleanor asked.

Vegas pondered some more. "Maybe. ... I wonder if Frisco plays chess."

"I'm confused," Eleanor said.

Vegas asked Bosco, "Have you ever heard of The Ponderosa?"

"Yeah," Bosco replied with disdain. "He was my brother's nemesis."

"Do you have any idea who he really is?" she said.

"Nobody knows," replied Bosco.

"Do you think Frisco Jones is The Ponderosa?" Eleanor asked.

"No, they don't have the same build. But I find it interesting that his name keeps coming up in our investigation. That can't just be a coincidence. I think I'm going to take this information to Sergeant Miller and see what he thinks."

22

Vegas, Eleanor, and Buttermilk arrived at the police station a little after noon. Vegas had wanted to go directly to the downtown Blue Falls station, but first, she had to get gas for her mother's vehicle, fill up the SUV to make sure it worked, follow her mother to her home, and argue about Eleanor staying put. As usual, she hadn't stayed.

"It's a beautiful day isn't it?" Eleanor asked.

"It's fine," replied a distracted Vegas.

"It's a good day to go shopping for shoes."

Vegas replied, "Shoe shopping? Why would today be a good day to go shoe shopping?"

"Every day is a good day to go shoe shopping," Eleanor said. "See, this is what you're missing by being obsessed with work all the time. You're missing out on all the fun of being a girl."

"I can't take time out for that, I have a case I have to solve."

"We could go shoe shopping and then go to a store that sells antique fashions and try them on," Eleanor suggested. "It would be fun."

Vegas thought it over. "I have to admit, it does sound like fun. But I can't have fun right now."

"Is that because you're with me?" Eleanor asked in a sad voice.

"That's not what I meant. I—" Vegas stopped in mid-sentence as she spotted Sergeant Miller getting out of his car about six parking spaces over. He had a cup of coffee in his hand and was walking toward the police station when he caught sight of Vegas, Eleanor, and Buttermilk and stopped. He stared at them like a gunfighter in an old Western movie trying to convince the cattle rustlers to leave with a stare.

"How did you know?" he asked.

Vegas and Eleanor had no idea what he was talking about, but they played it cool.

"Word gets around," Vegas said.

"Yeah," added Eleanor as she caught on to her daughter's act. "We know all about it. It's all over town now. We're here for the long haul, buddy, so spill the beans."

Vegas grabbed her mother by the arm as if to say that was enough. "Sorry, I got carried away," Eleanor whispered.

Sergeant Miller realized, "You two have no idea what I'm talking about, do you?"

"We don't know what a lot of people are talking about, to be honest with you," Eleanor said.

"The autopsy reports came in yesterday evening," he said.

"Were you going to call me?" asked Vegas.

"No," Sergeant Miller said in a matter-of-fact way.

"Why not? This is my case. I have a right to know."

"No, you don't," said the sergeant. "I don't have to provide police information to a private investigator. There's no court order or law that says that."

"But I thought we were a team," Eleanor said.

"We're not a team," replied the sergeant. "You know how in a pond all the leaves eventually get bunched together in the corner? We're like that. We don't belong together, we just happened to come together because of a bunch of strange weather currents."

"Well, if we're the leaves, then who is the pond?" asked Eleanor.

Vegas rolled her eyes and stared up at the sky praying the question could be wiped away from the world without anyone noticing.

"Would it be the apartment building?" Eleanor guessed.

"Never mind, Mom. What did the autopsy reports say?"

"Sanchez didn't have any smoke in his lungs, and—."

"So he's not dead?" interrupted Eleanor, which brought a blank stare from both the sergeant and her daughter.

"Is she for real?" Sergeant Miller said as he looked at Vegas.

"Somewhat," Vegas replied before she explained the

situation to her mother. "Since there was no smoke in his lungs, it means he was dead before the fire."

"Oh," Eleanor said. "But there was still a fire, right?"

Vegas decided her best path of action was to talk to Sergeant Miller and ignore her mother completely. "Do they know what he died from?"

"That's where it gets interesting. Sanchez and Cooter both had a toxin in their systems."

"Was it a drug overdose?" Vegas asked.

"No, poison," the sergeant replied.

"Poison?" asked a stunned Vegas. "What kind of poison was it?"

"Get this: It was toxin from a puffer fish," he informed them.

"What in the world is a puffer fish?" Vegas said.

"Some kind of poisonous fish that puffs up, hence its name," the sergeant said.

Eleanor's mind was racing. She knew she'd recently heard about puffer fish, but where? And who had said it? And why? And how come Buttermilk was so sleepy all the time, she wondered as she looked down at his sleeping form.

Vegas noticed that her mother was lost in thought. "What is it now?" she asked. "Don't tell me you had a pet puffer fish growing up."

"Okay, I know you all are going to think I'm crazy," Eleanor said.

"Mom, we know that you're crazy."

"Well, I've heard of a puffer fish before. Someone mentioned it recently, but I can't remember who."

"What do you mean? On TV or something?" asked the sergeant.

"Was it a documentary? The answer on one of your game shows?" Vegas added.

"No, it's not that," Eleanor said as she paced back and forth trying to jog her memory.

Vegas turned to the sergeant and asked, "Was he bit by the fish by accident or on purpose?"

"I would assume it was an accident when he was out swimming," the sergeant said. "How else could he get bit? They don't come as pets."

All of a sudden Eleanor yelled, "The pet shop, the pet shop!"

"What about the pet shop?" Vegas asked.

"I knew I heard of a puffer fish before! And when you mentioned pets, that made me remember. I'm so excited right now," Eleanor half-explained.

Vegas and Sergeant Miller shared a look.

"Are you having a spell or something?" Vegas asked.

"Not this time," Eleanor assured her. "When I went to the pet shop to get Buttermilk, the pet shop lady showed me a poisonous fish and said it was a puffer fish. I said no thank you to that, I'll take a dog, please. But they also had a beautiful parrot. It was also huge. I didn't realize they got that big! I don't think it was poisonous, but to be honest, I didn't ask, so I'm not sure."

"Okay, thanks, Mom," Vegas said and immediately asked the sergeant, "Do you remember seeing a fish tank in Jim Bob Cooter's house?"

"No. But his clothes were damp. Maybe he was out on a boat and got bit by one," he suggested.

"Do puffer fish live around here?" Vegas asked.

"They'd be in the water, honey," said Eleanor, which brought a sharp look from Vegas.

"Because if they do, I know someone who owns a boat," Vegas said.

"Who?" asked the sergeant.

"Frisco Jones."

"The owner of the Rhinehouse Apartments?"

"The one and only. Maybe Frisco Jones took Jim Bob Cooter out on his boat, and they went swimming and he got bit by one. Or maybe Frisco owns a puffer fish and he had it bite Jim Bob Cooter. Or it was a complete accident of some kind," Vegas concluded.

"If it was an accident, then why would they take him back to his house, lay him down in front of his bed, and turn the furnace on high? Something doesn't smell right," the sergeant said.

"Maybe it's all these fish," Eleanor said.

"What?" he asked.

"Never mind," Eleanor said and then asked Vegas, "Does Frisco Jones know Jim Bob Cooter? Why would he even meet him if he didn't even know he existed?"

"That's right," the sergeant said. "His son-in-law kept it a secret since Cooter wasn't supposed to be working there."

"Unless he found out," Vegas said. "Maybe he confronted him and things got out of hand."

"He confronted him with a puffer fish?" Eleanor asked.

Vegas thought it over. "I don't know how the puffer fish

fits into this equation. ... It doesn't seem to fit in any situation."

"It's very fishy," Eleanor added.

"We have to determine the last time Jim Bob Cooter was alive," Vegas said. "I know he was alive when we went to the Rhinehouse Apartments to see the security footage and he told me I couldn't."

"Can't the autopsy guy or gal be able to tell? That's how they do it on TV," Eleanor said.

"The coroner said that because of the heat being on so high, they couldn't get an accurate time of death," the sergeant said.

"I'd hate to have to pay his electric bill for this month," Eleanor added.

The sergeant looked at her with narrowed eyes. He just never knew what she would say next.

"Knowing that, and the bit about the puffer fish toxin, it sure seems like it wasn't an accident," the sergeant said.

"Exactly," Vegas said. "If it was an accident, you would take him to the hospital, not to his house, and lay him beside the bed and turn the furnace on."

"Unless you're trying to hide something," the sergeant added.

"Why didn't they put him on the bed?" asked Eleanor.

Vegas thought it over. "I don't know. Maybe the person couldn't lift him into the bed."

"I'll send a unit back to his house to look around again. Check the bed, look for any hidden safes, stuff like that," the sergeant said.

"I just had a fun thought. Well, not fun, seeing as how someone died, but you know," Eleanor said.

"What, Mom?"

"What if someone gave him puffer fish poison? Like made him drink it, or gave him a shot or something. I've seen that on TV, too."

"You've seen everything on TV," Vegas replied. "But that is the best idea you've had yet. Let's go to the pet shop and see if they've sold any puffer fish."

"Oh, Buttermilk can see his old home!" Eleanor said excitedly and rubbed Buttermilk's face. "Would you like that, sweetie?"

23

"**N**ow, you're sure that it was a puffer fish they had here and not a catfish or a praying mantis or something?" the sergeant asked Eleanor when the group met up outside Little Critter's Pet Shop.

"I'm positive," Eleanor replied. "I know it wasn't a catfish because I would have bought that, taken it home, and eaten it for dinner. I love catfish. And I have no idea what a praying mantis is. Is that a lizard?"

"Never mind about that, do you remember the name of the person that helped you in here?" asked Vegas.

"I don't think I ever got her name. She was Asian, though. Oh, no," Eleanor said as she placed her hands on both sides of her cheeks and a pained expression splashed across her face.

"What is it?" Vegas asked with concern.

"I called her *Asian*," she said. "Is that racist? I'm going to have to go to counseling now."

"No, Mom, it's not racist. It might not be a bad idea for you to go to counseling for other reasons, though."

"Can we just go inside?" a frustrated Sergeant Miller said.

The three of them walked into the pet store. There were all kinds of animals, and the cacophony they made echoed throughout the building.

"Do you see the woman that helped you, Mom?" Vegas asked.

Eleanor placed her hand against her forehead as she scanned the room looking for the woman, then said, "Ooh, over there!"

Vegas looked in the direction her mother pointed but didn't see anybody.

"Who are you pointing at? I don't see anyone over there," Vegas said.

"Right over there, that's the parrot I was telling you all about," Eleanor said excitedly. "It's beautiful, isn't it? It's about the size of an ostrich, though. I'd hate to have to clean his cage."

"We're not looking for a parrot, Mrs. Chantly," Sergeant Miller said.

"I know, but it talks. Just think about that — a talking animal! It doesn't sound real, does it? It sounds like something from a TV show. You know, that wouldn't be a bad idea — a sitcom about a talking parrot. It would get its person into trouble all the time by saying something inappropriate."

"Sounds familiar," Vegas said under her breath.

Eleanor pretended she didn't hear the comment. "And I guess they would have a crazy neighbor, too."

"Yeah, and it could fight crime at night," Vegas said jokingly.

"I would watch that," Eleanor said. "What should its name be?"

"Sergeant Miller."

"No, that name is taken. Remember that's this guy's name, honey? The guy standing right here?"

"No, I was talking to Sergeant Miller," Vegas said in frustration.

At that moment, the pet shop owner walked over to the three of them and asked, "May I help you?"

Eleanor realized it was the woman they had been looking for and immediately began shouting, "That's her! That's her!"

Vegas tried to calm her mother down as she said, "Okay, okay, this isn't a game show."

"Sorry. But it is her," Eleanor said in a whisper.

"I'm Sergeant Miller from the Blue Falls Police Department," the sergeant said as he shook the pet shop owner's hand.

"Is something wrong?" she asked with concern.

"No, ma'am, I just wanted to ask you a few questions. First, what is your name?" asked the sergeant.

"Stella Wong," she replied.

"That's an interesting name," Eleanor observed. "You sound like a character from a board game. She's in the billiard room with a candlestick," she added with a laugh.

"Mom, no," Vegas said in embarrassment.

"Uh, does this woman need help?" Stella asked.

"I'd have to say yes to that," replied the sergeant.

Vegas tried to get things back on track. "You're not in trouble or anything, Ms. Wong. We wanted to know if you have any puffer fish."

"I *did* have one, but I'm out of stock at the moment."

"How many have you sold since I bought Buttermilk?" Eleanor asked.

Stella looked at Eleanor like she was crazy. "We don't sell that here," she said.

Vegas interjected, "Buttermilk is the name of the dog you sold her, she's not here to buy actual buttermilk. Mom, why don't you go out to the car and drive off?"

"I remember you," Stella said as she examined Eleanor. "You're the one who wanted to eat my parrot."

Vegas stared at her mother in shock and practically screamed, "What?!"

"That was a misunderstanding," Eleanor assured her. "It was just meant as a conversation starter. We were just talking and uh, never mind, maybe we should get back to why we're here. You know, the puffin fish."

"Puffer," Vegas corrected, then addressed the owner. "When did you sell it?"

"I only had the one in stock, and I sold it after the dog. I can check my receipts for the actual date."

"Do you know the name of the person that bought it?" asked the sergeant.

"Yes," Stella said as she stepped behind the counter. "I should have the address as well. I also gave them some information on what to do in case they touch it."

"Touch it?" a confused Vegas asked.

"Yes, puffer fish can poison you just by touching them. Or eating them, as some people might want to do," she said and frowned at Eleanor.

"I thought they bit you, like a rattlesnake," the sergeant said.

"Oh, do you sell rattlesnakes? Maybe I'll get one of them next time. To scare off intruders," Eleanor said knowingly.

"Mom, stop," Vegas said, then asked Stella, "You mentioned them and they. There was more than one person?"

"Yes," Stella replied as she began punching the keys on her keyboard. "One came inside, and one stayed in the car. The one who came in went outside to talk to his friend when I told him the price. Then he came back inside and made the purchase."

"Do you have any security cameras in here?" the sergeant asked.

"No, the building owner said he would put some in, but he still hasn't. That corner over in the back also leaks when it rains, and he doesn't fix that either. Can I have him arrested for not fixing a leaky roof?"

"That's kind of out of my division," Sergeant Miller replied. "Talk to the building inspector, and they can tell you how to proceed."

"I remember our chimney leaked one time," Eleanor said to Vegas. "Your father fixed it by putting a big tarp over it. He was very handy."

"I hope he cut a hole in the tarp to let the smoke out," Vegas said.

"He did. Eventually," Eleanor said.

Stella clicked on something and said, "Here it is. He bought it the day after I sold the dog. Name of Jim Bob Cooter. Address is the Franklin Duplex on Eighteenth Street. Unit two."

"Eighteenth Street?" asked Vegas.

"Yes."

Vegas turned to the sergeant and said, "That isn't where he lives."

"He either has another place, or he just made it up," the sergeant replied.

Vegas thought for a moment and then asked Stella, "Who owns this building?"

"Frisco Jones," she replied.

Eleanor gasped.

"Have you ever met him?" Vegas asked.

"Just when I first rented the place," Stella said.

"What about your rent?" Vegas asked. "How do you pay it?"

"A security guard comes and gets it."

"Do you know his name?" asked the sergeant.

"No, sorry," Stella said.

"Have you always paid rent this way?" Vegas asked.

"Yes, but Mr. Jones initially told me to pay by electronic transfer. But when I signed the final lease papers, it said that the property security guard would collect the payments. So that's what I've been doing for the past two years. But no one came this month to pick up the rent. Does that mean it's free?"

"I don't know how that works out exactly," Sergeant Miller said.

"Well, they didn't come and get it, that's on them," Stella said.

"This security guard, is he around much?" asked the sergeant.

"He does some rounds a few times a week," she answered. "I think Mr. Jones has several properties, but only one security guard. He didn't seem like he was in too good a shape either, which seems strange to me."

"Did Jim Bob Cooter give any indication who the man in the car was?" Vegas asked.

"No. But it looked like they had a kid in the backseat though," Stella added.

"A kid?"

"Yes, I could barely see his head over the front seat."

"What kind of car was it?" asked the sergeant.

"I'm not sure, but it was an unusual-looking car," Stella said. "It looked like an older car."

"Any idea what model it was?"

"No, I'm afraid not. I'm not very good with cars. I just know pets."

"Too bad he didn't come in here on a bird. We would have had the perfect witness for that," Eleanor said with a laugh. No one joined Eleanor in laughing, so she just petted Buttermilk.

"Just out of curiosity," Vegas asked, "do you have a copy of your lease agreement handy?"

"Oh, yes. I have it right here so when he comes by for the rent, I'll show him he has to fix the leak in the ceiling. It says so under their maintenance clause, right here," Stella said and pointed to the line. Vegas was more interested in the signature, though, and asked to see the lease, then flipped to the last page.

"Okay, there, look at Frisco Jones' signature," Vegas said as the sergeant and her mother looked over her shoulder. "There's a line just above it. It looks like a photocopy, not the actual signature."

Vegas handed the lease back to Stella.

The sergeant said, "Okay, let's go check out Jim Bob's new place first. And then I think we need to have a talk with Frisco Jones."

"Don't mention they haven't collected my rent yet!" Stella yelled after them.

24

The sergeant's car pulled up in front of the Franklin Duplex, followed almost immediately by Vegas, Eleanor, and Buttermilk in the Trans Am.

They all exited their vehicles and looked at the duplex, which seemed to be better-taken care of than the Rhinehouse Apartments building.

"Which number is it again?" Vegas asked the sergeant.

"Unit two. Looks like that's the one on the right there," the sergeant pointed out.

Vegas started toward the unit when Sergeant Miller grabbed her by the arm and said, "Hold on now."

"What's wrong?"

"I'm waiting for backup before we go in."

"I thought we were your backup," Eleanor said.

"No," replied the sergeant. "You all are my problem."

"Problem might be overstating it a little, don't you think?" Vegas asked.

"I want to make sure we have enough enforcement on the scene in case something goes wrong," the sergeant informed them.

"But isn't Jim Bob dead?" Eleanor asked.

"Yes, but someone killed him," the sergeant reminded her. "They could be hiding inside. So let's just play it safe until Blue Falls' finest gets here, okay?"

"Sure," Vegas said.

They didn't have to wait long before a Blue Falls Police motorcycle drove up. It was driven by a female officer clad in what appeared to be full combat gear. On the back of the motorcycle was a male officer in his standard uniform with his arms wrapped firmly around the woman's waist, as if he was terrified of falling off.

"What in the world?" Sergeant Miller said at the sight of two officers on one motorcycle.

The motorcycle riders removed their helmets, placed them on the seat, and walked to the sergeant and stood at attention.

"Hello, Sergeant Miller," Officer Cody Perkins said with a salute. "I got a call that you needed some backup. I'm honored that you asked for me."

"I didn't ask for you," Sergeant Miller said bluntly. "I just said send somebody."

"I'm somebody, sir," Officer Perkins said.

The sergeant examined the officer for a moment and said, "You're not a motorcycle officer. In fact, you're barely an officer of any classification."

"They moved me to the Blue Falls Highway Patrol division a few days ago. They had an opening for motorcycle officers because of that tragic accident involving the hot sauce truck. I applied and they took me right in," Officer Perkins said. He then introduced his fellow officer, "This is Officer Mary Ross."

"It's an honor to meet you, Sergeant Miller," Officer Ross said with a firm handshake that seemed out of place with her small stature.

"I don't believe I've met you before. Officer Ross, was it?" Sergeant Miller said.

"Yes, sir. I entered the force through the diversity lottery," she replied.

"The what?"

"The diversity lottery," she continued. "They have a lottery for people who are underrepresented in the police department."

"So you got this job because you're a woman?" asked Sergeant Miller.

"No, sir, I got it because I'm short."

"We're looking for short people for the police force now?" the sergeant asked.

"Not anymore, sir," Officer Ross said. "That position is filled. By me," she added proudly. She gave a snappy salute, and the sergeant asked, "Did we run out of motorcycles?"

"No, sir," Officer Perkins replied. "Why do you ask?"

They all just stared at each other for a moment until Vegas broke the awkward silence. "Then why are you both riding the same motorcycle?"

"I forgot mine again," Officer Perkins said.

"You forgot yours?" asked a perplexed Sergeant Miller.

"Again?" Eleanor added.

"Yeah. I was very excited and confused when I found out Sergeant Miller asked for me. I'm a big fan of yours, Sergeant Miller. So when Officer Ross got on her motorcycle, I just jumped onto the back of hers. It's a little easier for me, anyway. I'm still not that good at riding them — I knocked the mirror off of one of the patrol cars yesterday."

"It's really safer for everybody if he just rides with me," Officer Ross confirmed.

At this point, Vegas noticed that Officer Perkins' holster was empty and asked, "Where's your gun?"

Officer Perkins looked down at his empty holster, and panic blanched his face. "Oh, crap. I bet that's why all those cars were blowing their horns," he said to Officer Ross.

Eleanor, Vegas, and the sergeant all dropped their jaws in shock. After a moment, the sergeant took a deep breath and sighed, then turned his back and threw his hands in the air.

"What exactly do you need me to do?" Officer Perkins asked the sergeant.

"I just called in to have some backup. I was hoping they would send some actual officers," he replied with a stare.

At that moment, a man came out of unit two. The group watched in shock as he closed the door, locked it, and proceeded to walk past them. Sergeant Miller stopped him before he walked away.

"Excuse me, I'm Sergeant Miller with the Blue Falls Police. Do you live here?"

"No, I'm a real estate agent. Reggie Mullins," he said and pulled out his card, and handed it to the sergeant. "Say, are you and your large and very diverse family interested in buying this place? It's pet-friendly," he added, looking at Buttermilk.

The sergeant was offended. "These strange people are *not* my family. That's a whole different group of crazy people. ... We were given this address for Jim Bob Cooter's residence."

"I'm afraid that he passed away, which is why I'm here. The duplex is available to buy or rent if you're interested. Good rates available! The other unit is occupied by a little old lady if you would like to talk to her."

"That might be a good idea," Vegas said.

"She's not here right now. She went to Las Vegas on vacation."

"She went to Vegas, Vegas!" Eleanor shouted. "I've always wanted to say that. It's why I gave you that name, actually."

"Just for a joke?" she said incredulously.

"It was worth it," Eleanor said proudly.

Vegas shook her head. "Do you know when she'll be back?" she asked Reggie.

"About twenty years. I heard she got arrested," he replied.

The sergeant mumbled, "I feel like I'm in a *Saturday Night Live* sketch in which the cue cards got all mixed up." Then he told Reggie, "We would like to go into Cooter's unit and have a look around."

"Sure, no problem," Reggie said and led them to the unit. "Are you all police?" he wondered.

"I'm a private investigator," Vegas said.

"I am, too," Eleanor said. "I'm her mom."

"Well, how cute," Reggie said. "A mother and daughter detective squad."

"We're thinking of making a TV show about our lives," Eleanor responded.

"We are?" Vegas asked.

"I'd watch it," Perkins said. "Wouldn't you Ross?"

"It depends on what night it's on," Officer Ross replied. "I bowl on Tuesdays, so if it's on Tuesdays, then I wouldn't watch."

The sergeant said, "I'm drowning in weird people right now." He turned to the agent and asked, "Can we look inside now?"

"Sure thing, boss." Reggie unlocked the front door. "Don't mind the mess, the cleaning crew hasn't been in yet. It's a two bedroom, one bath, great location. Let me know if you're interested."

Eleanor raised her eyebrows and nudged Vegas as if to tell her to buy it, but Vegas just shook her head.

It was a home of the basics. A living room, a kitchen, and a narrow hallway leading to the back, where the two bedrooms and bathroom were located. The house was still furnished. It looked like Jim Bob Cooter had just gone out to the store and would be back any minute.

"Why would Jim Bob have two homes?" Vegas asked.

"And how could he afford it?" Eleanor added.

"They're only two miles apart from each other," the sergeant said. "It doesn't make any sense for a single guy to have two houses. If he was married, then I'd understand."

"Are you selling the unit for Jim Bob Cooter's relatives?" Vegas asked Reggie.

"Nope. This is owned by Frisco Jones. He owns a large number of properties in the area. I've been instructed to put the unit up for sale or rent whenever it becomes vacant."

That fact piqued Vegas' interest, and she momentarily filed it away as she walked around the living room and then headed into one of the bedrooms. It was well-kept, and the bed was made. She opened the closet and found some men's clothes hanging up. She looked around but didn't find anything interesting, and then got down on her knees to look underneath the bed. There were the usual dust balls, but she also found a box. Vegas slid it out. It was about four feet long by three feet wide. She sat on her knees and began to open the box.

Just then, Sergeant Miller, Eleanor, Buttermilk, and Reggie walked into the bedroom.

"What's in the box?" the sergeant asked.

"Just this," Vegas said as she pulled out a black cape, mask, tights, and boots.

"What's that?" asked Reggie.

"This is The Ponderosa's outfit that I saw at the chess tournament, but it couldn't have been Jim Bob wearing it because he was already dead," Vegas said as she tried to fit the pieces together.

"Wait, who was wearing it? What chess tournament? Why is it in Jim Bob's house? I'm a little confused right now," the sergeant asked.

"Welcome to my world," Eleanor said.

25

The motley crew consisting of Vegas, Eleanor, Buttermilk, Sergeant Miller, and the dynamic motorcycle duo of Perkins and Ross arrived at the Blue Falls Marina in their various vehicles and assembled on the pier.

"Frisco Jones' boat is down here in boat slit fifteen," Vegas informed them.

"Maybe he can shed some light on everything that is going on here," Sergeant Miller said as they headed toward the boat slit.

"He has to be involved somehow," Vegas said. "Everything keeps coming back to him in some form."

"He seemed so nice when we met him the other day," Eleanor said. "I just can't believe he's a criminal."

"Being nice doesn't mean you're not a criminal," Officer Perkins said.

"He also seemed too old to be a criminal," Eleanor replied.

"Being too old doesn't mean you're not a criminal," Officer Perkins said.

"Fifteen is right over here," Vegas said. It was empty.

"Looks like he's gone out," Sergeant Miller said.

"What do we do now?" Officer Ross asked.

"Should we swim out there and look for it?" Officer Perkins said.

"Yeah, why don't you do that, officers," the sergeant said facetiously. Officer Ross started to undo her shirt but was quickly stopped by the sergeant.

"Stop that!" he said. "We don't need anybody jumping into the water. Especially in their birthday suits."

"It's part of the job, sergeant," Officer Ross said.

Sergeant Miller examined the empty boat slip and said, "Maybe he knew we were coming."

Just then Vegas noticed a security officer walking toward them. She thought he looked familiar.

"Hello," he said. "Are you all waiting for Mr. Jones, too?"

"Oh, you're the guard from the Rhinehouse Apartments," Vegas said.

"Yep. I was supposed to meet Mr. Jones here today. He said he'd be here all day."

"Well, he's not here," said the sergeant.

The guard looked at the officers and asked, "Is he in some sort of trouble?"

"Possibly," the sergeant answered. "We want to talk to him about some things. But you'll do in the meantime. Why were you supposed to meet him here?"

"He called and told me he wanted to talk to me, that's all," Jennings said.

"Do you know anything about Jim Bob Cooter?"

"Just that I had him fill in for me. We weren't the greatest of friends or anything like that."

"Did you know he had two places of residence?" Vegas asked.

Jennings gave a dumb look and replied, "No."

"When was the last time you saw him?" Sergeant Miller asked.

"It was the day you all came to look at the security footage. He said he had to go and deal with some things. I told you all that."

"Do you have any idea what he was dealing with?" Vegas said.

"No, he just left, and that was the last I saw of him. I've been trying to call him for some time, but he never answers the phone. Maybe he left town."

Vegas was startled that he didn't know about Jim Bob and blurted out, "Jim Bob Cooter is dead."

A look of horror came across the guard's face. "Dead? You mean like dead dead, or like dead on his feet?"

"Dead dead," Vegas replied.

The guard took his hat off and ran his hand through his hair over and over. "I can't believe it. Is it my fault? I called him to fill in for me. Do you think Mr. Jones killed him?"

"Do you? He is your father-in-law," Sergeant Miller said.

Jennings looked uncomfortable. He shifted his weight

and then stammered, "I, I, well, I thought with you all here, that's what you thought."

"Do you have any reason to believe Frisco Jones would have killed Jim Bob Cooter or Billy Sanchez?" he pressed.

"No, I, well, like I said, I thought that's why you were here. I didn't mean to imply anything," Jennings said.

The sergeant asked, "How did Mr. Jones react when he found out you had been hiring another security guard while you went off skateboarding and such?"

Jennings was obviously no longer paying attention. A distracted look crossed his face, and he blurted out, "I better, I got to go."

The guard took off running.

"Hey, get back here!" the sergeant yelled. He turned to Officer Perkins and ordered, "Stop him!"

Officer Perkins turned to run after the guard and immediately tripped over a raised plank on the decking and fell into the water with a loud splash.

Sergeant Miller shouted, "He didn't go that way, you idiot!" Then he took off after Jennings. He chased him up the pier and into the parking lot but quickly lost sight of the security guard; he was too far ahead. The sergeant headed back to the pier.

"Did you find him?" Vegas asked after she helped Officer Perkins out of the water.

"No, he got away," said the sergeant. "You okay, Perkins?"

"I'm just wet, sir."

The group decided to head out, and as they did so,

Vegas noticed an elderly man with a full gray beard and a captain's hat sitting in a lounge chair nearby.

"Excuse me, but do you know the man who owns the boat over here?" Vegas asked.

"Frisco Jones?" the man said. "Yeah, we've known each other for fifty years. Went to school together. Is he in some sort of trouble?"

"We're not sure. What's your name?" Vegas asked.

"Ollie Rush. I'm retired. Single, too, if you're interested," he said with a wink.

Vegas threw up a little in her mouth and said, "No, I'm good. Is there anything you can tell us about him?"

"He's not here."

The sergeant joined the questioning. "We can see that. Do you know where he went?"

"He said he was going out to meet another boat for a party. He's a big party guy now. His wife died a few years back, and he began letting his employees run his company — he owns properties all over Blue Falls — and went full gusto into the party circuit. I'm not big into parties myself. I'd rather just hang out in my boat by myself."

"Did he say when he'd be back?" Vegas asked.

"I asked him that," replied Ollie. "He had a big smile on his face and said in a couple of days but that a week wasn't out of the question."

The sergeant turned to Vegas. "A week? Something tells me that isn't a good sign. He may be making a run for it."

Vegas asked Ollie, "Was he by himself?"

"He had another fellow with him, kind of scrawny,

nerdy. He irritated me, to tell you the truth. He acted like he was something big and important. There were also some little people with him."

"Little people?" Vegas asked.

"Yeah, you know, dwarves."

"That's going to be some party," Eleanor said.

"Did Frisco say who they were?" Vegas asked.

"Security. Said the tall one was his new head of security because of some chaos at his properties," Ollie said as he pulled a can of soda out of the blue and white cooler at his feet, popped the top, and took a big gulp that was chased with an "ahh."

This comment caught the attention of everyone in the group. Even Buttermilk, who woke up from his umpteenth nap of the day.

"What kind of chaos?" asked the sergeant.

Ollie said, "He'd been having some financial problems and couldn't figure out why. Accounts weren't adding up right or something."

Vegas thought Ollie seemed lonely, which she knew from experience meant the person was more likely to keep talking, so she prodded him with a simple "Why?" He burped and continued.

"Excuse me. Once he took to being the party guy, he didn't pay much attention to the company, I guess. He just assumed everything was paid into his bank account. That's how he fixed everything up. Each month his tenants would make a payment electronically, on the computer. I don't exactly know how computers work, to be honest with you. I don't own one myself.

Seem to be more trouble than they're worth if you ask me."

Vegas turned to the sergeant and said, "We talked to Bosco earlier, and he said all the tenants in the building would pay their rent to the security guard each month. Just like the pet shop owner was instructed to do. Frisco wasn't paying much attention to the business, so they forged his name on the lease agreements, and all the rent money went straight to them when they collected it."

Eleanor asked, "But if they paid by check, it would have had Frisco's name on it. How could they have got the money then?"

"They just forged the endorsement signature on the back of the checks, too, and deposited them into a different account," Vegas said.

"He probably kept writing checks or making payments on things believing the money was in the account," thought the sergeant.

"They send out monthly bank statements," Eleanor said. "At least that's how they do at my bank. Unfortunately, their statements are depressingly accurate."

Vegas tried to make sense of everything running through her head. "Someone else must have given him the bank statements and changed them. Or just created one on the computer and showed him that."

"But what would that have to do with Wilson?" asked Eleanor.

"Maybe he found out about it," Vegas said. "Then he was going to tell either the police or Frisco Jones."

"That could get someone killed, all right," said the

sergeant. "I'll contact the Coast Guard and have them watch for Jones' boat. Do you know the name of it?"

Vegas thought for a moment. "Something about Christmas. ... Oh, it was Frosty!"

"Frosty? Who in the world names their boat Frosty?" the sergeant said, shaking his head. "I'll radio it in." He headed back to his vehicle.

"Should we rent a boat and go out looking for him?" Eleanor asked.

"No, he could be anywhere," Vegas replied.

"Too bad you don't have a drone," Officer Perkins said as he tried to dry himself off with his handkerchief.

"Drone?"

"Yeah. You could go out a way in a boat and then fly it up into the sky and look around for miles. It would increase your range dramatically."

"If only we had a drone. We just have a dog," Eleanor said.

"I know someone who has one," Vegas said. "Let's go."

26

"I don't understand," Eleanor said and looked at her daughter as if she was wearing a horse head at a funeral.

"Good. Then everything's normal," Vegas replied as she pulled into her mother's driveway.

Eleanor sighed, looked at her house, then said, "I thought we were going to Bosco's."

"We are."

Eleanor looked through the Trans Am's windshield and asked, "We are at my house, right?"

"Yes."

"So we're going to Bosco's apartment the long way?" Eleanor asked in a drawn-out voice.

Vegas smiled and said, "No, I just want to take your SUV instead of my car."

"Why?"

"I don't think I have room for three people, a dog, and a drone. Your SUV is bigger."

Eleanor nodded and said, "Okay, I think I understand now."

"Good," Vegas said.

"But I have to be honest with you."

"What's that?"

"I don't really want Bosco in my vehicle."

"I don't want him in mine, either," Vegas said. "But you wanted to be a detective, so we're going to use your Yukon. Now, let's go."

Vegas walked to her mother's SUV and tried to open the passenger's-side door, but it was locked. She turned to her mother and saw her struggling to get Buttermilk out of the Trans Am.

"Come on, boy," Eleanor said in baby talk. "Your sister wants to use Mommy's vehicle instead of hers, so you have to take your nappy-nap there."

Eleanor got Buttermilk out of the car and set him on the ground as Vegas said, "The door is locked, Mom."

A worried expression crossed Eleanor's face. "Oh, dear," she said and began rummaging through her purse. "I have no idea what I did with my keys." She pulled out a piece of paper. "There's that coupon for that manure I got the other day! I knew I had it, but I couldn't find the stupid thing in the checkout line. They're always trying to hurry you up."

"Hurry up, Mom."

Eleanor looked at her and saw she was joking. "Very funny, dear. Now, where are they? ... I think I took them inside and set them on the kitchen counter."

Vegas glanced at the front door and asked, "Didn't you lock the house?"

"I don't know. Let's find out!" Eleanor said and walked to the front door and tried to turn the handle, but, like the SUV, it was locked.

Vegas came up behind her and said, "That's not good. Maybe we can go through one of the windows in the back."

"That's very smart, and you know why? Because that's what your father would do when we got locked out of the house. Ideas must be genetic, too."

"Did that happen a lot?" Vegas asked.

"Once you're past forty, things that you don't want to happen seem to happen a lot," she said sagely.

They walked to the back of the house and saw that the laundry room window was halfway open.

"That's kind of high," Vegas said.

"That's not even supposed to be open," Eleanor said. She looked around and saw something else out of place. "And why is your father's saw horse on the ground?"

"Maybe Buttermilk knocked it over," Vegas said.

"Well, let's see if we can fit in," Eleanor said as she stared up at the laundry room window.

"We?" Vegas said. "You can't get up there. It's too high."

"Well, I might need a running start, but I think I can do it. How long of a run do you think I'll need?"

"Maybe start in Boston. Do you have a ladder?"

"Oh! It's in the outbuilding," Eleanor said as she pointed with a thumb over her shoulder at a small barn-like building. It sat on cinder blocks against the wooden fence that bordered the property along with tall, thick pine trees.

The two of them headed to it, and Vegas opened the doors, which squeaked and groaned like the doors of a haunted house.

Light filtered in and washed over the large collection of miscellaneous items that had piled up over the years. There basically was no room to maneuver inside the building because of all of the stuff that was littered about.

"What a mess," Eleanor said as she looked past Vegas. "Your father would be so upset with me for letting it get this way."

"I don't think Dad really kept it that clean, either," Vegas said as she stepped over a push mower and grabbed the ladder that was hanging on the wall by two long nails.

"Yeah, but he knew where everything was," replied Eleanor.

Vegas maneuvered the ladder out of the barn and took it over to the laundry room window.

"You be careful now," Eleanor said.

"I will. Just hold the ladder so it doesn't slip."

Eleanor stood on the bottom rung of the ladder to help hold it in place as she watched her daughter climb up.

"If you feel like you're going to fall, just jump into my arms and I'll catch you," Eleanor said.

Vegas looked at her doubtfully. "Um, sure, Mom, I'll do that."

Vegas got to the half-open window and was able to push it open all the way. She climbed through the window and landed safely on the laundry room floor.

"I'm in," Vegas shouted out.

Eleanor shouted back at her, "You know, you're disturbingly good at breaking into houses."

Vegas stuck her head out the window and saw her mother starting to climb the ladder. "What are you doing?" Vegas screamed.

"I'm climbing up the ladder so I can get in."

"Well, stop!"

Eleanor stopped on the ladder, looked up at her daughter, and in all innocence said, "But the front door is locked."

Vegas shook her head. "I'll go unlock the front door so you can come in that way."

"But we already have the ladder out."

"I don't want you to climb the ladder, Mom. A good daughter doesn't let her mother climb ladders to get into the laundry room. Now, go around to the front door and I'll open it."

Eleanor looked down from the second rung. "To be honest, I am getting queasy. Either I'm scared of heights or I'm pregnant."

Vegas looked down at her mother and asked, "What did you say?"

"I'm going around! And you might have a baby sister soon!" Eleanor shouted back.

Eleanor climbed down the ladder and went around to the front of the house. "Sister?" Vegas mumbled. "What is she talking about? I wonder if I need to put her in a retirement home soon."

Vegas started to head to the front door when she saw a piece of fabric hanging up on the window sill. It looked like it was part of a red shirt, and it definitely wasn't hers. She looked around and saw that the washing machine had been pulled out, and a rope was tied around it.

Vegas exited the laundry room slowly, walked down a small hallway that led into the living room, and almost fell over with shock at what she saw.

The place had been ransacked. Items were strewn about. Cabinet doors were opened. Drawers were pulled out, their contents were thrown onto the floor. The couch cushions had been unzipped and the foam support cushions inside exposed. Even a portion of the wall had been ripped down, taking with it part of the ceiling.

She heard a knocking sound and froze, but quickly realized it was her mother at the front door. Vegas hurried over to it and opened it.

"What took you so long? I hope you started a load while you were in the laundry—" Eleanor gasped as she noticed the mess.

"Someone has broken into your house, Mom," Vegas said.

"Oh, my goodness, I hope they didn't get that new package of bobby pins I just got."

"Your main concern is bobby pins?"

"They were unopened. I love opening up a new package of bobby pins. Makes me feel good for some reason," Eleanor said as her eyes scanned the house. "And, gracious, do I ever need to feel good right now!"

Vegas and Eleanor made their way through the house and tried to see if anything was missing. But after looking for around forty-five minutes, the only thing they could say that had been taken was their sense of security.

"To be honest, it's kind of insulting," Eleanor said.

"How's it insulting?"

"They didn't think any of my stuff was worth stealing. I have a lot of valuables in here."

"Yeah, I know. The bobby pins."

"Maybe it was a bunch of kids doing a prank," suggested Eleanor. "The college isn't too far from here, so maybe they chose my house as the prank house. That's a little encouraging."

"How's that encouraging?"

"It explains why they didn't take anything. They just wanted to make a mess."

Vegas looked around some more and said, "I think the people that broke in were looking for something specific. I'll bet they used the sawhorse to get up to the laundry room window and came in that way. There's a rope tied around the washing machine, which makes me think there was at least one more person involved who wasn't as athletic as the first one."

"Maybe it was the criminal's mother," Eleanor said in a bolt of inspiration. "Maybe they're our exact opposites. Instead of fighting crime as a mother-daughter duo, they *commit* crimes as a mother-daughter duo! Or father-son. Or father-daughter. Or even mother-son!"

"Yes, so many possibilities," Vegas said and rolled her eyes. "We better go check my place, too."

Not long after, they arrived at the camper park. The door to the camper was wide open. Vegas got out of the vehicle and was running to the camper when her mother shouted, "Be careful! Someone might still be in there!"

Vegas entered her home cautiously, but no criminals popped out of the mess. Her place had been ransacked as well.

Eleanor entered and shook her head. "I guess we can rule out pranksters. Should we call the police?"

"Not yet," Vegas said.

"Why not?"

"This has to be about the case. Somebody is looking for something, and I've got to figure out what it is."

"Maybe they're giving us a warning that we better stop investigating or the next thing they mess up will be our beautiful faces," Eleanor said.

Vegas looked at her mother seriously and placed her hand on her shoulder. "I have to be honest with you — you could be right. I told you this could be dangerous."

They both stood there looking at the destruction. The initial shock wore off and they realized what it meant. Their homes, the places they went to for comfort, rest, and security, had been violated. They both felt fear, sadness, and anger.

"Why would people do this?" Eleanor asked.

"Some people just don't care. They want something, and it doesn't matter how they get it," Vegas said.

"But we didn't take anything from anyone," Eleanor said.

"They obviously think we have something."

Eleanor raised her chin, and a determined look crossed

her face. She wasn't going to let them scare her, and it was time to do something, time to go into Mom Mode.

"So what do you think? Is this about the Wilson Hopkins case or just some burglars with attention deficit disorder," Eleanor said.

"Attention deficit disorder?" asked Vegas.

"They didn't take anything. They just went around tearing things up."

Vegas shook her head. "I think it's part of the case. Now, let's go find a killer."

27

E leanor drove herself, Vegas, and Buttermilk to the
Rhinehouse Apartments.

"I think we should call the police," Eleanor
said for what seemed like the twentieth time.

"Later, Mom," Vegas said.

"I think you're being bullheaded on this. Like you think
only you can figure out everything. The police have more
resources than you do," Eleanor reprimanded her daughter.

Vegas thought over her mother's words. "Okay, maybe
you're right. I just don't like people I care about having
their house broken into. It's one thing to do it to me, but it's
something else when they do it to you."

Vegas stared out the open window as the highway wind
washed over her. She felt alone for the first time in a long
time.

Eleanor said, "Honey, you're acting like your job is to
protect me."

"It is," Vegas said. "You and Dad took care of me when

I was younger. Now I'm supposed to take care of you. I guess the truth is ..." she paused. "Well, I feel like I failed you when your house got broken into."

"I understand what you're saying, honey. I feel the same way about you. I want to protect you extra hard because your father passed away."

They both tried to keep their tears inside and held hands, realizing how much they meant to each other.

"We're kind of a mess right now, aren't we?" Vegas asked.

"I guess we are. But we'll get through it."

Vegas laid her head back against the headrest, then sat up straight and said, "Here's the plan: We'll go to Bosco's, then we'll stop at the police station. Deal?"

"Deal," Eleanor replied as she spit in her hand and offered it to Vegas to shake.

"What are you doing?" Vegas asked in disgust as she stared at her mother's hand.

"Sealing the deal. This is how gangsters do it."

"I think that's the way ten-year-old boys do it," Vegas said. Eleanor didn't remove her hand, and Vegas sighed and spit in her own hand and shook her mother's to seal the deal.

"Now, how exactly is Bosco going to help us again?" asked Eleanor.

"He's got the drone. We'll take him to the marina and have him launch it and see if he sees any sign of Frosty."

"Do you think it can really find the boat?"

"It's a long shot. If he's way out, then it'll be no good. But we have to try. With the Coast Guard looking, too, we can at least find out where the boat isn't. Also, we have to get this done before dark or we won't be able to see anything."

When they arrived at the Rhinehouse Apartments, they headed directly to Bosco's apartment. They knocked on the door repeatedly, but there was no answer, not even after Eleanor yelled "Rumpelstiltskin!"

"Do you think he's been kidnapped?" asked Eleanor.

"I don't know what to think right now."

They headed back down the stairs and stopped at the security office. Vegas knocked on the door several times, but again, no one answered.

"Is today national hide from Vegas day?" Vegas wondered.

She then tried the doorknob, and it turned.

"We shouldn't go in there," Eleanor said.

"I don't think anyone is in here."

"That's why you shouldn't go in there," Eleanor said. "We could get into serious trouble doing this, you know?"

"I'm on a case with my mother and her dog. I'm already in trouble."

Vegas slowly walked into the small office.

"Hello? Is anyone here?" she called.

She saw several computer screens, which she assumed were for the security cameras, but they were all off. There was a half-eaten pizza and an open soda can on the desk.

Vegas observed, "Looks like someone left here in a hurry."

"Did they see us coming?" Eleanor asked.

"It's possible."

"I think it's time to talk to Sergeant Miller."

"You're right. Maybe the fact that Bosco and the security guard are gone is related, and maybe the police can help. Let's head on down to the station. Sergeant Miller also can tell us if the Coast Guard found the boat," Vegas said.

They got back in the SUV and headed to the police station. On the way there, they passed the warehouse where they had been held by the security team a few nights ago. It seems like weeks ago, Vegas thought, and then caught sight of someone near the warehouse's east wall.

"Pull over in that parking lot!" Vegas yelled, which caused her mother to immediately swerve into the other lane and into the parking lot.

"What was that?" Vegas asked as the SUV came to a stop and they tried to catch their breaths.

"You yelled to pull in here, so I pulled in here."

"I didn't mean to go all Richard Petty here," Vegas said.

"Oh, I just love his music!" Eleanor replied.

"No, that's Tom."

"Tom who? Is he a suspect?"

"Never mind," Vegas said, trying to focus on the case. "I saw somebody over at the warehouse."

"So?"

"I want to check it out," she said.

"But that could be anybody," Eleanor said. "I think the stress of this case is getting to you. Here, hold Buttermilk — he's like a therapy dog."

"No, thanks. I'm going to go check it out. You wait here."

"Yeah, that's not happening," Eleanor replied.

All three got out of the vehicle, and Vegas ran to the edge of the parking lot where she had a good view of the warehouse. There, on the left side, was a person draped in black like some sort of ninja. Vegas started to walk to the warehouse when Eleanor grabbed her by the arm and said, "You can't go over there."

"Why not?"

"Because it could be dangerous."

"Dangerous is my middle name," Vegas said.

"No, your middle name is Diane. I named you myself," Eleanor said.

"Diane means dangerous in Latin," Vegas said as she hurried across the road. Eleanor and Buttermilk trotted behind her trying to keep up.

Vegas got to the corner of the warehouse and saw that the man dressed like a ninja was tangled in some blue rope. He struggled a bit and then tore off his mask in frustration. She relaxed as she saw who it was. "Bosco?" she said aloud.

"Don't hurt me, I'm delicate!" Bosco screamed in surprise.

Everyone looked at each other and said at the same time, "Why are you here?"

Vegas took the lead and said, "I'm here because I saw you over here."

"How did you see me?" asked Bosco. "I'm wearing black."

"Um, it's daylight out," Vegas said.

"What is this outfit anyway?" Eleanor asked.

"It's my ninja outfit. My brother and I were planning to start a ninja boy band."

"You're a little old to be in a boy band, don't you think?" Vegas asked.

"Hence the outfits," Bosco said as if she should have realized that.

Vegas looked at his outfit tangled in rope and couldn't help but ask, "Did you break into my mother's house?"

"Of course not. Why would you think that?" he said with a twisted face.

"Because you're breaking into the warehouse," Vegas replied.

"If I broke into anyone's house, it would have been yours."

"Someone did break into my house," she said.

"Why would you think I did it?" Bosco asked.

"Because you just said you would."

"I didn't mean that I did it. Who broke into your house?" Bosco said.

"I don't know. But why did you say that you would break into my house?"

"Because I think I'm falling in love with you," Bosco said and turned away shyly. "There, I said it."

"Oh, God," Vegas mumbled as she looked up at the sky and checked to see if the apocalypse had started yet.

"I think that's sweet," Eleanor said.

"I don't want you to break into my house whether you love me or hate me," Vegas said forcefully. "And us ain't happening. I don't date clients. Unless they're hot. Now, why are you all tangled up in this rope?"

"I tried to throw it up on that window there, but I missed and it fell on me and scared me, and I started fighting it and got all tangled up. I know it sounds odd, but that's what happened."

"Oh, it sounds quite plausible to me," Vegas said. "But why are you throwing rope up at a window?"

"You said you saw the chess set in here, and I'm going to get it back. It's about time that I become a man and fight for what's mine. Well, technically it's my brother's. But—"

His speech was cut off by a loud scream.

"What is it?" Vegas said.

"Sorry, I saw a huge spider," he said and sniffled, trying to hold back tears. "I just want to be a real man," he said sadly.

"And you are doing a great job, Bosco," Eleanor said encouragingly. "Even Rambo is afraid of spiders."

"Not as much as me," Bosco pouted.

"Well, yes, that's true, but that was a very big spider, wasn't it?"

"The biggest!" Bosco said.

"Okay, enough about spiders," Vegas said. "Next time you see one, just let me know and I'll squish it. Now, why are you trying to get into the window up there anyway? First off, there are windows down here at ground level. Secondly, did you try the front door? It is daytime, you know."

"A ninja wouldn't go the easiest route," Bosco said.

"You're not a ninja," Vegas said bluntly. "C'mon," she said and led the group to the front. They entered the building with no issues and didn't see a single person. Which made it eerie, Vegas thought.

"I'm scared yet very excited," Bosco said as he looked around the hallway. "I've never broken into anything except for a vending machine in high school."

"You're still not breaking in — we entered through the door," Vegas said. "Okay, the office where I saw the chess set is just over here."

They looked inside the office and were shocked by what they saw: The desk was overturned, its contents and other papers were strewn around the room, a lightbulb was broken, and a shelf was hanging by a screw.

"Well, we know where the people went after they left our homes," Eleanor said.

Vegas and Bosco walked into the room, picking through the mess to try and find the chess set. Vegas looked up to ask Bosco a question when she saw something.

"What's that thing over by you?" Vegas said.

"Ah, a body!" Bosco screamed and promptly fainted.

"Is he okay?" Eleanor asked from the doorway.

"He'll be fine," Vegas said, noticing he landed on a pile of papers. "This one, on the other hand. ..."

The body was lying face down against the wall. Vegas walked to it and rolled it over. It was the security guard, William Jennings.

"Is he dead?" Eleanor asked.

"No, he's not dead," she said, feeling his pulse. "But it looks like he got beat up pretty good."

"Who did?" Jennings asked weakly.

"Shh, just stay still. We'll get an ambulance," Vegas said.

"It wasn't supposed to be like this. No one was supposed to get hurt," Jennings mumbled.

"Who did this to you? What's this all about?" Vegas asked.

Jennings stared up at Vegas, "You're the girl investigator."

"Yeah, who did this to you?"

"What did you do with it?"

Vegas looked at him, puzzled. "What do you mean? Do with what?"

He passed out again from his injuries before he could respond.

Just as one passed out, another awoke — Bosco slowly rose up and asked, "What happened?"

"You fainted. Just dropped like a sack of potatoes!" Eleanor said.

"Do you have a cellphone?" Vegas asked him.

"Yeah, here," he said, handing it to her. Then he coughed dramatically and said, "You know, I might need mouth to mouth."

"That's what the dog is for," Vegas said as she called 911.

28

Sergeant Miller pulled up outside the warehouse where Vegas, Eleanor, and Bosco stood. Buttermilk was lying on his side absorbing the final hour of sunlight as if he was a furry solar panel. Sergeant Miller got out of his car, walked over to the odd-looking trio, and asked, "What is he wearing?"

"This is my ninja outfit," Bosco said as he rubbed the fabric.

"Okay, that just brings up more questions, so I'll ignore that and ask: Why are you all here?" Sergeant Miller said.

"I came here to get my brother's chess set, but it's gone," Bosco said.

Sergeant Miller looked puzzled as he asked, "What chess set? And why is it here?"

Vegas explained. "When my mother and I were held here, I saw a gold and silver chess set. Turns out it belonged to Wilson Hopkins."

"Wilson was my brother," Bosco said. "He had a blue ninja outfit just like this one, by the way."

Vegas shook her head at Bosco with a tight-lipped expression. He got the hint and continued. "I don't know why it was here, but the chess set belongs to me because I inherited it after my brother's death. So it's not legally stealing then."

"Do you own the building?" asked the sergeant.

"Well, not in so many words," Bosco mumbled.

"You can't just go into a building and snatch something in there that you think belongs to you. You're not O.J. Simpson," the sergeant said.

"That's neither here nor there," Vegas said. "There's a man inside who was beaten up pretty good. And it happens to be one William Jennings."

"Well, that certainly is interesting. Any idea why he was here?" the sergeant asked.

"I don't know. ... Wait!"

"What is it, honey? Do you have to go potty?" Eleanor asked.

"No, Mom. I think the security guards were looking for the chess set. My mother's house and my camper were both broken into sometime today, and the office here, where the set had been, was ransacked, too."

"Why would they look for that at my house?" asked Eleanor. "I can't play chess. I'm a checkers girl."

"Maybe they realized the set was missing and thought me or my mother took it when we were here," Vegas said and turned to her mother. "Remember that they went upstairs looking for Buttermilk and when they came back down I had found Buttermilk in the office? Between then and whenever they looked for the chess set, it wasn't where they had left it, so they thought one of us had it."

"What's so great about this chess set?" the sergeant asked.

"It's worth a million dollars," Bosco said.

"That could lead to murder, all right," the sergeant said. He turned to Eleanor and Vegas and asked, "Do you two want to go down to the police station and file a report about your homes being broken into?"

"Right now I want to go to the marina and use Bosco's drone to see if Jones' boat is anywhere in the area," Vegas replied.

"If he has the million-dollar chess set, then that boat is long gone by now," the sergeant said. "I'd wager he realized he had financial troubles and needed a lot of money quickly, so he stole the set. I doubt we'll ever see it again."

"Never?" Bosco said, his eyes widened in shock.

"I'm afraid not," replied the sergeant. "Now, why don't you two come down to the police station and file reports. I'll send some units to your houses to have a look around. Since the break-ins appear to be related to the case, maybe we can find something that will help us."

Eleanor and Vegas agreed and were about to leave when Bosco asked, "Do you still want to try the drone?"

"You have it with you?" Vegas asked.

"Yeah, I thought I might be able to use it to get the chess set back," he replied.

"Can you show me how it works? I'd still like to use it at the marina."

"Sure," he said and got the drone from the scooter. He set it on the ground near Vegas and powered it up. He touched the controls and it shot straight up. Vegas looked at the screen on the controller.

"As you can see, I'm very good at this. I'm what you call a professional pilot," Bosco bragged.

"You're flying a pretend plane, not a real one," Vegas said.

"It's not as easy as you think. Do you want to try it?" Bosco said and handed her the control when she nodded yes.

Vegas began flying it around, hovering it over the warehouse. Something caught her eye on the roof.

"What's that?" she asked.

Bosco, Eleanor, and the sergeant crowded around the screen to look. It appeared to be a large tarp spread out with something setting on top of it.

"Fly it lower so I can see what that is," instructed the sergeant.

As Vegas tried to fly it lower, she suddenly lost control, and the drone crashed into the side of the roof, bounced off, and landed in a tree.

"You have some Amelia Earhart tendencies there," the sergeant said. "How do we get to the roof?"

"There's a fire escape on the other side," Vegas said as she handed the control back to Bosco with a hasty apology.

"How am I going to get that down?" Bosco asked as he looked into the tree.

Meanwhile, Sergeant Miller and Vegas ran up the fire escape and onto the roof. As soon as they were on the roof, a strong stench hit them, and they both covered their noses and mouths.

"I hope that's not a body," Vegas said.

"It sure does smell like it," the sergeant said from under a hand he was using as a gas mask.

They saw something on the tarp and slowly approached, hoping it wasn't a body part.

"What the?" the sergeant said.

"Puffer fish!" Vegas said. There was a pile of the poisonous fish, and they looked like they had been dissected. "Now we know for sure it wasn't an accident that killed Jim Bob and Sanchez."

"But why are they here on the roof? Just sitting here to rot and stink."

Just then, a seagull flew overhead and squawked. Vegas offhandedly looked at it.

"That's it," she said.

"What's it?" asked the sergeant, looking at the sky where she was.

"They put the evidence on the roof for the seagulls to eat," Vegas said. "But they apparently didn't know what the pet lady told us, that the puffer fish are poisonous. No wonder there's still a pile here — the gulls wouldn't touch them."

They both stared down at the fish for a moment. Then the sergeant said, "I'll get somebody up here to secure the scene. And let's make sure officers check out your homes before you go back in."

"Why, Sergeant Miller, you do like us after all," Vegas said with a smile.

29

The police units did a sweep at Eleanor's house first. They searched for any evidence that might help identify the intruders, took some photos, processed the rope that was found tied around the washing machine, took DNA samples, and dusted for fingerprints. Then they went to Vegas' camper and did the same thing.

"What a day," Eleanor mumbled when the police team finally left and the women had picked up their homes.

"Yeah, thanks for helping me clean up," Vegas said.

"You helped me clean up my place, so I helped you clean up yours," Eleanor said cheerfully. "I think it's even cleaner than before the bad guys got here. Although there's still an awful lot of things lying about."

Buttermilk wandered over to Vegas' bed with a pathetic look on his face, and Eleanor picked him up and placed him on the bed.

"Don't put him on the bed, Mom."

"It's okay, he won't fall off."

"That's not what I meant. I don't want dog hairs all over me."

"Honey, you've had dog hairs on you ever since I bought Buttermilk."

Vegas looked at her clothes and began picking fur off them.

"I wish I could have used that drone down at the marina," Vegas said.

"I have to agree with the sergeant: That boat is long gone and not coming back. You're better off letting the police handle it from here on out," Eleanor said as she picked up some stray dishware and placed them in the cabinet. "Besides, that drone thing helped you find those fish on the roof. So technically you did get to use it."

"Yeah, until I crashed it. And I know what you and the sergeant said is true, but I was hired to solve this case, and that's what I'm going to do."

"But your investigation showed that Wilson was murdered, that it wasn't an accident. Someone obviously killed him to get the chess set." Eleanor picked up a pair of skimpy underwear and looked at her daughter and exclaimed, "Vegas! What have you been doing?"

Vegas humped her shoulders, "Sometimes I want to feel like a woman."

"You should be trying to feel more like a lady instead," Eleanor said in her mom voice.

"Give me that," Vegas said as she swiped the clothing out of her mother's hands and placed it in one of the nightstand drawers.

Eleanor sat down on the bed beside Buttermilk and began petting him.

"Did any of your neighbors see anybody come into your camper?" Eleanor asked.

"I'm really the only full-time resident here," Vegas said as she looked at her alarm clock and was disappointed to see that the plastic lens was cracked. "Most people just come here for the weekend or for holidays."

"My neighbors didn't see anyone break into my house either. Whatever happened to having nosey neighbors? That's what we need more of today: neighbors with binoculars who want to see what's happening next door."

"Uh, I don't know if we want to go that route," Vegas said as she sat down in her patio chair.

"Do you want to go out for something to eat?" Eleanor asked.

"I'm not really hungry."

"You haven't eaten all day. You're getting skinny as a rail."

"I'm fine, Mom. I wonder where Frisco Jones is," she said, changing the subject. "I can't help but feel I'm missing something."

"Maybe he was in on it to start with. Wouldn't you have noticed that your bank account wasn't matching what the books were saying? I think so. He had to be in on it," Eleanor concluded.

"I think someone else is involved."

"Why?"

"William Jennings said something odd at the warehouse. He said, 'It wasn't supposed to be like this.' What does that mean? Did they accidentally kill Jim Bob, Sanchez, and Wilson? Is there a part I'm missing?"

"What does the fish being on the roof mean?"

"They put them up there for the birds to eat, to destroy all the evidence, but it didn't work," Vegas said.

"What would it even matter if someone found dead fish? For heaven's sake, they could have just thrown them anywhere. No one would have thought it was attached to a crime," Eleanor said.

"It's like the sergeant said, when people commit a crime, they don't think straight and make mistakes. Putting the fish on the roof for the seagulls to eat was a good idea for them at the time. They didn't think about a drone finding them," Vegas said. "They could have eaten them as well."

"Don't you remember, puffer fish are poisonous?" Eleanor said.

"The pet store owner said she was surprised you didn't want the puffer fish since you wanted to eat the other animals, and—"

"Oh, goodness, it was a joke!"

"Well, anyway, she said if they're fixed right, you can eat them." Vegas sat up straight as she had a thought. "Hey, that's where they got the other fish. They weren't purchased just from pet stores! Someone could have bought them from restaurants. Or they work for a restaurant and have access to them."

"How many restaurants in Blue Falls serve puffer fish?"

"Let me see your cellphone," Vegas said. Eleanor

handed it over and Vegas began searching for restaurants that served puffer fish.

"You really need to get your own phone," Eleanor said. "You're the only twenty-seven-year-old I know who doesn't own a cellphone or a computer. You're like a computer atheist or something."

"I'll be fine," Vegas said distractedly.

"I don't see why anybody would want to eat a puffer fish. If they want to eat something dangerous, then they should eat five cans of chili beans. There's nothing in this world more dangerous than five cans of chili beans."

Vegas glanced at her mom and was about to ask her how she knew that but decided not to open that can of worms. She looked down at the phone and said, "I found one. It's called the Red Dragon. The proprietor is James Wong."

"That's interesting," Eleanor said.

"How so?"

"Wong is the name of the pet shop owner."

Vegas looked at her mother, both surprised and impressed. She pondered the information for a moment, trying to fit all the pieces together. Then she said, "I'm calling the restaurant."

Vegas began dialing as Eleanor said, "What are you going to ask them?"

"I'll think of something," Vegas said as she waited for someone to pick up on the other end.

"Oh, you should disguise your voice," Eleanor said. "You always did a good SpongeBob Squarepants."

Vegas shook her head and held up a finger to silence her.

"Red Dragon, how may I help you?"

"Yes, I was wondering if you serve puffer fish," Vegas asked.

"We do, but we are out of stock at the moment. Our kitchen was broken into a few nights ago, and all the puffer fish were stolen right out of the live tank."

"Stolen?" Vegas' mind began turning over scenarios. "I'm sorry to hear that. Did someone break in?"

"Yeah, they apparently got in through a small vent in the kitchen. I don't know how in the world anyone would fit through it, but that's the only way they could have gotten in. We do expect a fresh supply next week, though, so be sure to come by then."

"Thank you, I will. Goodbye."

"What did they say?" Eleanor asked.

"All their puffer fish were stolen. Someone broke in through a small vent in the kitchen, which makes no sense."

Vegas got to thinking. When she went in through her mother's laundry room, she had to raise the window to get in. However, someone had already gotten in and out of the window without having to raise it more than it was positioned. That meant that it had to be somebody small. Even the little people were involved, she concluded.

"What are you thinking about over there?" Eleanor asked.

"I think this is turning into a huge operation on several different fronts."

"How so?"

"There appears to be embezzlement, murder, chess, rental properties, disappearances, breaking and entering, stolen property, and puffer fish poisoning. One person alone couldn't do all of this. There has to be a gang involved here."

"So what are you saying?"

"We need to find Frisco Jones."

"How in the world are we going to do that? He's at a big party now. A party that could be anywhere in the world," Eleanor said.

"What if it's not a party? The old man said another man was with him."

Vegas stood up and handed her mother's phone back to her. "We need to do a stakeout."

"A stakeout? Where?"

"The one thing missing right now is Frisco Jones and his boat," Vegas said.

"That's two things, actually," Eleanor as she petted Buttermilk.

"I think we should go to the marina and see if he shows. Let's go."

30

Vegas and Eleanor were stationed near the boat slips, hiding in the SUV. They could see the water well enough to spot anyone coming back.

It was one o'clock in the morning, and Vegas was hunched down in the passenger seat peering through her binoculars. Eleanor was loudly eating potato chips from a large bag while she read the *Guinness Book of World Records* by flashlight. Buttermilk had assumed the Buttermilk Position — lying on his side asleep.

"Do you have to eat so loudly?" Vegas asked as she put her binoculars down to glare at her mother.

"I wouldn't be making any noise if you had let me get a hot dog like I asked," Eleanor said.

"Where did you get those chips anyway?"

"I keep them in the back for Buttermilk. He likes to have a salty snack every now and then. And so do I," she said and again crunched down on a chip. Vegas shook her head in annoyance.

"How long does a stakeout take anyway?" Eleanor asked.

"As long as necessary. Now be quiet and turn off your flashlight."

"I can't read without a light. I don't have that superpower."

Eleanor was about to comply, but then she dropped a chip and attempted to retrieve it. As she did, she accidentally bonked the vehicle's horn with her forehead. The resulting honk seemed loud enough to wake the dead. "Sorry," Eleanor said and reached for the chip again but set her other hand on the horn and accidentally pressed it several times, which caused Buttermilk to start barking.

"What are you doing?" Vegas asked in an upset whisper.

"Mommy's sorry, but I got my chip, so everything is fine," Eleanor said as she untangled herself from the steering wheel and held up the chip, illuminating it in her flashlight beam.

"I don't think enough people heard us," Vegas whispered angrily. "Why don't you go ahead and light some fireworks, too?"

"I had to get the chip. I don't want my vehicle dirty. Then I got hung up on the horn. It's my first stakeout, so you should give me a little slack. Okay?"

"What are you reading?"

"The *Guinness Book of World Records*. It's very inspiring. Here's one guy that can catch watermelons with his mouth."

"That's impossible."

"Nothing's impossible if you apply yourself. It says here that he caught seventeen in a row. They dropped them from a five-story building and he caught them in his mouth. Wait, that doesn't seem right," she said and read the entry again. "Oh, it's just seeds. He catches watermelon seeds in his mouth. It doesn't sound as impressive now, does it?"

"You need to be quiet," whispered Vegas.

"And you need a husband," Eleanor whispered back.

"Mom ..."

"You started it," Eleanor said before she turned away and ate another chip.

Vegas just shook her head in disbelief. She had once had a nightmare that was eerily similar to this stakeout. She lifted her binoculars and looked toward the open water when she was startled to see a person step into her view.

"Ahh!" she screamed, which caused Eleanor to accidentally hit the horn again. The person outside yelled, "Don't toot!"

"Pepper?" Vegas asked as she calmed down and got a good look at the person.

"Hey, Vegas. How's it going?"

"Why are you here?" Vegas asked.

"Your mother emailed me and asked me to help with your stakeout."

Vegas turned to her mother in confusion and asked, "Why did you do that?"

"I thought it would be a good idea to have a man around. You know, in case of trouble," she replied, and then addressed Pepper. "Did you have any trouble finding us?"

"No, I heard your signal."

"Signal?" Vegas asked.

"Yeah, the horn toots," Pepper said and got into the backseat with Buttermilk.

"Come in," Vegas said sarcastically.

Pepper crinkled his nose and sniffed. "I smell manure."

"It's our vehicle, we'll pass the time however we want," Vegas replied.

Pepper looked over Eleanor's shoulder. "What are you reading, Eleanor?"

"Shh, be quiet," Vegas said as if she was a kindergarten teacher.

"It's the *Guinness Book of World Records*," whispered Eleanor. "I'm thinking about entering it."

"That's great," Pepper whispered back. "I had an uncle that tried to set the record for eating oysters."

"How many did he eat?" asked Eleanor.

"Four," Pepper said.

"That doesn't sound like very many," Eleanor said.

"He choked on a pearl and died before he could finish," Pepper said matter-of-factly. "He didn't set the record, but at least we got to keep the pearl."

"Oh," Eleanor replied, horrified at the news.

"Yeah," he said. "Hey, can I have a chip?"

"Sure, but we have to be quiet or Grandma will get mad at us."

"Would you two be quiet?" Vegas said.

Eleanor looked at Pepper as if to say, "See?" and then offered him the bag of chips. He took a handful and began munching them loudly.

"Mmm, these are good," he said.

"They're Piggy's Potato Chips," Eleanor informed him. "They use real artificial ingredients."

"Hmm," he said, nodding. Then he asked Vegas, "Have you seen anything yet?"

"Shh!"

"Hey, so, um, Vegas, do you want to get a bite to eat after this?" he asked.

Vegas ignored him and kept looking through the binoculars.

"Uh, Vegas, did you hear me?" asked Pepper.

"No," Vegas said.

"No you didn't hear me, or no you're not interested in eating?" he asked.

"I'm interested in eating, but not with you."

"Well, technically we're eating together now," Pepper said as he ate another chip.

"No, technically you're eating with my mother. Maybe you should date her," Vegas replied.

Pepper looked at Eleanor, who said, "I'm touched that you want to go out with me, dear, but it wouldn't work out. I've seen how you keep your house."

Suddenly Bosco knocked on Eleanor's window, which brought screams from everyone inside the SUV.

"What are you all doing?" Bosco asked.

Eleanor rolled down her window. "It's a stakeout!"

"For the record, this is not how a stakeout goes," Vegas chimed in.

"Can I play?" Bosco asked.

"We aren't playing," Vegas said. "Besides, I thought you went home."

"I was going to, but got to thinking that I should come down here and look around, and then I found you thanks to your signal."

"Oh, for the love of— It wasn't a signal, it was just my mom accidentally honking the horn," Vegas said.

"Hi, I'm Pepper," Pepper said, offering his hand.

"And I'm salty," Vegas said.

"I'm Bosco."

"I really enjoyed your brother's chess book."

"You play chess?" Bosco asked.

"Sure do! I'm playing in the Reno tournament in a few weeks."

"Me, too. Have you made your costume yet?"

At this point, Bosco climbed into the vehicle to continue the conversation and sat next to Buttermilk and Pepper.

"I'm going as a bishop this year," Pepper said. "How about you?"

"A castled king."

"Oh, that's brilliant," Pepper said as he leaned back with his hands on top of his head. "I wish I'd thought of that."

"Yeah, I've never seen it done before. I just hope my head fits through the hole. Hey, chips."

Eleanor offered the bag of chips to Bosco, and he took a fistful. Just as he did, they all saw lights out on the water. It was a boat, and it was heading straight for the slits. As it entered the marina, Vegas could tell that it was the Frosty.

"There it is," Vegas said in a loud whisper.

"Let me see," Bosco said as he pulled the binoculars from Vegas and peered through them.

"It's the Frosty, Frisco Jones' boat. And I'm the only one allowed to look through the binoculars," Vegas said as she pulled the binoculars away from Bosco.

"Vegas, share your toys," Eleanor said.

Vegas angrily shot back, "It's not a toy!"

Suddenly, there was another knock at the window, and they all screamed. Sergeant Miller poked his head in through the driver's window and asked, "What are you all doing?"

After Vegas caught her breath and realized who it was, she said, "We're on the worst stakeout in history."

"What are you staking out?" asked the sergeant.

To which everyone in the vehicle said, "The Frosty."

"At least everyone is focused," he replied.

"Why are you here?" Vegas asked.

"I wanted to see if the boat came in yet."

"It just did," Vegas told Sergeant Miller.

The boat had docked, and three little people and a man with a box in his arms got off the Frosty.

"Who's the tall guy?" Vegas said.

Bosco grabbed the binoculars from her and looked through them. "That's Ronald McDonald. He was the other janitor for a while, then he disappeared."

"Oh, lord, him," Vegas said, remembering how he had hit on her at the chess tournament.

"He's a real person?" asked a stunned Eleanor.

"Not that Ronald McDonald, Mom."

"*That's* Ronald McDonald?" the sergeant asked in

surprise. "He's known around the precinct. He's a petty thief. Did you know him, Bosco?"

"A bit. My brother played chess with him at his apartment for a couple of weeks."

"I know him, too," said Pepper. "I've seen him at several chess tournaments. He's a clown."

"You shouldn't make fun of people because of their name," Eleanor scolded.

"I mean, he was a joke. He couldn't even play chess. He kept trying to jump the pieces, like in checkers," Pepper explained.

Bosco added, "My brother got him disqualified from one tournament because he was using a mirror."

Vegas, Eleanor, Pepper, and Sergeant Miller all looked perplexed at this bit of information, and the sergeant was about to ask how a mirror would help when Vegas said, "You're going to have to explain that to us later. Right now, we've got to wrap up this case and stop McDonald before he puts away that box. Let's go!"

Soon the group was headed toward Ronald McDonald and his three little followers. McDonald spotted them and yelled, "Run for it, boys!" McDonald and his friends took off down the pier but stopped after a short way when they realized they weren't going to outrun Vegas and her group.

"Help, help, police!" Ronald McDonald shouted as he covered his head in anticipation of being hit.

"I'm the police," Sergeant Miller said.

"Man, that was fast," McDonald said. "I've just been attacked, and I want this street gang arrested."

"What's in that box, McDonald?" asked Vegas.

McDonald looked at the box in his hands but then asked, "Wait a minute, how do you know my name?"

"You tried to pick me up at the chess tournament the other night?" Vegas said.

"Oh. Are you still interested?" he asked.

Bosco suddenly shouted "hiya!" and karate chopped McDonald's arm, which caused him to drop the box.

"Oh, my god, I think I broke my wrist!" Bosco yelled as he danced around nursing his wrist.

The others looked at the box. Some of its contents had fallen out, and Vegas could plainly see they were Wilson's special chess pieces.

"That belongs to Wilson Hopkins," she said.

"No, it doesn't," McDonald said nervously. "I won this at the Des Moines chess

tournament."

"Des Moines doesn't even have a chess tournament," Pepper said.

"It doesn't? Are you sure? Well, then ... attack!" McDonald yelled to his friends.

The three little people got into karate stances and started to advance on the group.

"What do we do now?" Eleanor asked. "I haven't been in a fight since that one Christmas sale when I bit—"

"Never mind, Mom, just stay on your feet," Vegas instructed her. "Wait, what?"

Suddenly a motorcycle came charging down the pier. On it was Blue Falls' strangest cop duo, Perkins and Ross. Perkins jumped off the back of the motorcycle and tried to draw his gun, which unfortunately wasn't there, and instead shouted, "Freeze! Or my partner will run over you!"

Ronald McDonald wasn't about to comply and began to run, but he tripped on Buttermilk's leash and crashed to the deck.

Sergeant Miller shouted, "Hold these — what do you all like to be called? Little people? Dwarves?" he asked them.

"We're just people," one of them said.

"Perkins and Ross, hold these people!"

The duo captured the trio, and the others rushed over to McDonald, who was desperately trying to untangle himself.

"See that, Vegas?" Eleanor said. "It's not so easy getting untangled from a leash."

Vegas ignored her and grabbed McDonald by the shirt collar. "Did you kill Wilson Hopkins?"

He panicked. "No. Well, maybe, yeah. No! I'm sticking with no. I mean it was an accident."

"Explain," Vegas said, jerking him by the shirt.

Ronald took a deep breath and began spilling the beans. "I bought Hopkins' book to help me with my chess, but it didn't help. I kept losing and got tired of everyone laughing at me."

"You probably should have just changed your name," Eleanor said.

"Mom, no," Vegas said with a shake of her head.

McDonald continued: "Also, trying to hypnotize people gave me a headache. So I went to his apartment to confront him. He wasn't there, so I got Jim Bob Cooter to let me in. I waited for Wilson to come back. I could hear him upstairs with his brother. I think they were wrestling."

They all looked at Bosco.

"It was Friday night," Bosco said and shrugged his shoulders as if everyone should have known that.

"Then he came down and I lost my nerve, so I hid in the closet," McDonald said. "Then I fell asleep because it was dark, and when I woke up, he was vacuuming. So I thought that was my chance and I charged out of the closet, but I accidentally knocked him down. When I heard he had died, I panicked. So I got Billy's hat and placed it in the closet to try and, well, you know, make it look like he did it. But I didn't mean it in a bad way."

"So that implicated Jim Bob in the murder as an accessory, so he erased the security footage," Vegas deduced. "What else, McDonald?"

He looked at Vegas and admitted, "Okay, there isn't a chess tournament in Des Moines."

"Where's Frisco Jones?"

"Well, he's somewhere in the ocean," McDonald said.

"For someone with such a happy name, you sure do a lot of killing," Eleanor said.

He frowned. "Well, Jones found out that we were embezzling from the company. We knew the gig was up, so I had to inject him with puffer fish poison. The guys stole the fish from the restaurant. We wanted as much puffer poison as we could get to make sure we did the job right."

"Who was The Ponderosa?" asked Vegas.

"William Jennings. I was his manager. We hired some goons to be his bodyguards and got the outfit for him to create intrigue. He was great at chess and kept getting better. I never could do that."

"So Jennings really hired Jim Bob Cooter to fill in for him?" Vegas asked.

"Yeah. He introduced me to the little people, and I brought them into the gang. Everything was going great, and we were making money. I was somebody! I mattered! Then Jim Bob Cooter wanted out, but he knew too much. I had to take him out. It's how it's done," he said with a shrug.

"Why did Jim Bob have two homes?" the sergeant asked.

"He liked to brag to people that he owned two places. But of course, he didn't," he said. "I also had problems with him taking The Ponderosa outfit without permission. He liked wearing it around his house at night. Kind of creeped us all out."

There was silence while everyone pondered this new information, and then suddenly McDonald yanked himself free of Vegas and made a run for it, yelling, "You'll never take me alive!"

Sergeant Miller pulled out his gun and fired a warning shot. McDonald immediately dropped to his knees and screamed, "Don't shoot! Don't shoot! I'm too young to die!"

"You're coming with me," the sergeant said as he picked up McDonald off the ground.

"Wait," Vegas said and then addressed McDonald: "Why did you kill Billy Sanchez?"

"He heard us talking about what happened and said he was going to snitch to the police. I couldn't allow that," he said. "I injected him with some poison and then tried to make it look like a fire. Who in the world checks for puffer fish poison anyway?"

"Blue Falls' finest is who," the sergeant said as he took McDonald to the police car and, with the help of Perkins and Ross, locked him in the back with the little people.

Bosco turned to Vegas with a huge smile on his face. "I don't know what to say other than thank you. You have a great team here, thank you!"

Vegas looked at her mom and smiled. "I love it when a plan comes together."

31

The sun warmed Vegas and her mother as they walked hand in hand up a winding path in the cemetery. Buttermilk trailed behind them, only awake because he could smell something fun in the picnic basket Vegas carried.

They headed to a small concrete bench with the words "God is with thee" engraved on its seat. They sat down in front of John Chantly's grave and took a moment to remember him. The past came alive inside their minds, and neither time nor distance separated them for a while.

The sunlight fell in and out of the trees as a breeze rustled its branches like a quiet rain. The ladies soaked it in, and Eleanor looked up and in the distance saw some birds that looked like they were drawn onto the dark-blue sky.

"It's so peaceful here isn't it?" Eleanor asked.

"It's lovely," Vegas said. "With the trees and the quiet, it's like you're miles away from the city."

They sat still for a few seconds, neither knowing what

to say. Eleanor leaned her head on her daughter's shoulder and tried not to cry as she whispered, "He would be so proud of you."

"Thanks, Mom," Vegas replied. "He would be proud of you, too, you know." She softly put her head against her mother's.

After a minute, Eleanor stood up and said, "Well, I didn't come all the way up here just to cry. Let's have us a Hardee's sausage and biscuit and some hash browns in honor of your dad."

Vegas smiled. "One sausage and biscuit and hash browns coming up."

Vegas reached inside the picnic basket and pulled out the biscuits. She unwrapped one and was about to hand it to her mother when Buttermilk snatched it right out of her hand. Eleanor and Vegas laughed as he gobbled it down.

"He sure does like buttermilk biscuits," Vegas said. "Looks like you named him the right thing."

Eleanor laughed again and placed her hand into Vegas', and the tears began to fall softly. They sat together holding each other without saying a word.

To learn more about the author Kyle Owens, and to be notified when the next Vegas Chantly Mystery is released, visit OffBeatReads.com.

Milton Keynes UK
Ingram Content Group UK Ltd.
UKHW010725200923
429044UK00001B/21